BEST SELLER ROMANCE

A chance to read and collect some of the best-loved novels from Mills & Boon—the world's largest publisher of romantic fiction.

Every month, three titles by favourite Mills & Boon authors will be re-published in the *Best Seller Romance* series.

A list of other titles in the *Best Seller Romance* series can be found at the end of this book.

Kay Thorpe

BITTER ALLIANCE

MILLS & BOON LIMITED
15–16 BROOK'S MEWS
LONDON W1A 1DR

All the characters in this book have no existence outside the imagination of the Author, and have no relation whatsoever to anyone bearing the same name or names. They are not even distantly inspired by any individual known or unknown to the Author, and all the incidents are pure invention.

The text of this publication or any part thereof may not be reproduced or transmitted in any form or by any means, electronic or mechanical, including photocopying, recording, storage in an information retrieval system, or otherwise, without the written permission of the publisher.

This book is sold subject to the condition that it shall not, by way of trade or otherwise, be lent, resold, hired out or otherwise circulated without the prior consent of the publisher in any form of binding or cover other than that in which it is published and without a similar condition including this condition being imposed on the subsequent purchaser.

*First published in Great Britain 1978
by Mills & Boon Limited*

© Kay Thorpe 1978

*Australian copyright 1978
Philippine copyright 1979
Reprinted 1979
This edition 1985*

ISBN 0 263 75133 3

*Set in Linotype Times 10 on 11½ pt.
02–0685*

*Made and printed in Great Britain by
Richard Clay (The Chaucer Press) Ltd,
Bungay, Suffolk*

CHAPTER ONE

'I HEAR Tristan's taking you up to the country seat this weekend,' said the girl at the filing cabinet without turning her head from what she was doing. 'Going to be vetted by big brother, are we?'

Jaime's eyes went involuntarily to the sparkling diamond on the third finger of her left hand, still not fully accustomed to the sight of it nestling there. She smiled a little. 'I doubt if eight years' seniority makes him that much of an ogre. Tris seems very fond of him.'

'He'd have to be, wouldn't he. The man holds the family purse strings.'

'Tris is hardly reliant on family hand-outs,' refusing to be drawn too far by the thinly veiled jibe. 'After all, he's a director here at Lockharts.'

'A very junior one, with rather expensive tastes.' The pause was deliberate, the glance round hinting of malice. 'But maybe you'll manage to change him.'

A smile and a shrug was Jaime's only answer. It should have been from the first, she acknowledged. Nothing she could say was going to make Gwen Walsh see her as anything but the character she herself had painted. Jealousy wasn't a pretty emotion, especially when it was allowed free rein. Not that the other girl had ever held any claim on Tristan Caine. Two dates didn't actually start a relationship.

Three certainly had with her, though, she reflected as the office door closed behind the other girl. Barely six weeks since she had started this job, and here she was engaged to be married to her boss already! Life held many surprises, not least among them being the discovery that behind that jaunty, man-about-town exterior there lurked a man of real worth. Tris was fun to be with, but he had his serious side too. It had come to the fore when he asked her to marry him, overlaying the teasing sparkle in the blue eyes.

'There's only Liam and me left to carry on the Caine line,' he had said. 'I'd like to see our kids grow up round Oakleigh.'

Jaime's look had been uncertain. 'Is that the only reason you want to get married, Tris?'

'No,' he said, and the sparkle returned as he swung her closer into his arms. 'I want a lifelong secretary I don't have to pay!'

It was some time later before Jaime had got round to asking how he intended to bring up any children in Derbyshire while working in London.

'Simple,' he said. 'We have a little time to ourselves— say a year or so—then as soon as it starts to happen we move up to Derbyshire permanently. It was always planned that I go back and help run the estate eventually. As a qualified accountant I'll be in a perfect position to take over from the present estate manager when he retires, and I'll still be under thirty.'

Jaime said blankly, 'Just how big is the place, Tris?'

'Oh'—he shrugged—'big enough. There's the house, plus three farms supplying the business.'

'Business?'

'Dairy produce. We have our own chain of retail outlets in most of the towns within a fifty-mile radius. Then there's Liam's horses, of course. He's a well-known breeder. Never heard of the Oakleigh Stud?'

'No, but that's nothing to go on. I never had anything

to do with the horse world.' Jaime looked and felt more than a little bemused. She had known Tristan came from a well-to-do home, but until this moment no one had seen fit to fill her in on the actual details. Probably it had been taken for granted that she was fully conversant with them already. She tried to rationalise. Why should it alter anything? Love was supposed to transcend all barriers, wasn't it? True love, at any rate.

She came back to the present with a brief jolt as the outer door opened once more to admit the object of her thoughts. The boyish, handsome face belied his twenty-six years, as did the grin which crossed it at the sight of her sitting there.

'Slacking again, Miss Douglas! How about earning that huge salary we pay you and bringing your book in for some dictation?'

'Yes, sir,' Jaime returned demurely, and gathered her things to follow him, laughingly protesting as he swung the door closed behind her and pulled her to him. 'Not in working hours!'

'It helps me to concentrate,' he said, and kissed her anyway, holding her a little away from him after it to look down into her wide browed, clear-skinned face under the long, thick mane of coppery hair which defied all attempts at fashion styling. 'You're good for me, Jaime. You give me inspiration.'

Green eyes met his with a smile in their depths. 'Not judging from that letter you gave me earlier for Rutledge and Co. I had to rewrite two thirds of it.'

'Why else do I keep you on?'

He kissed her again, briefly this time, then moved away to his desk under the wide window overlooking St Martins Le Grand. 'I'm going to be out to lunch and for most of the afternoon. Lucky we decided to travel Saturday morning instead of going up tonight.'

'Isn't it!' Jaime looked up from her book. 'You're supposed to be seeing Mr Rodgers at three-thirty. Do you want me to put him off?'

'Might as well, considering. I might be back, then again I might not. You know what these big accounts are like. They're our life's blood, but they certainly want value for every pint!'

He dictated steadily for twenty minutes or so with one eye on the clock, pushing back his chair at the end of it with a sigh of relief.

'That's that for now. The rest can wait a week till we get back. Can't imagine how the old firm will run without its mainstays!' He reached for his briefcase, selecting certain papers from the small pile on the desk and pushing them into the folder Jaime handed across to him. 'See you tonight?'

'It wouldn't be a bad idea to have an early one if we're setting off at nine on the dot,' she pointed out practically. 'Besides, I still have to pack and do last-minute jobs around the flat.' She hesitated a moment, before tagging on with a certain diffidence, 'What sort of clothes am I likely to need?'

'Oh, nothing special. We stopped dressing for dinner years ago, unless there's something on.' The smile was fleeting. 'I suppose there's always the chance Liam will have arranged an engagement party for us.'

Jaime said quietly, 'You never really told me how he took the news. I mean, it must have been a bit of a shock hearing it over the phone right out of the blue like that.'

There was something faintly evasive in the sudden interest Tristan seemed to be taking in one particular paper. 'He was surprised, naturally, but you can't shock my brother very easily. He's looking forward to meeting you.'

Jaime wished she could say the same of him. Liam Caine was an unknown quantity, and not one she particularly wished to plumb. Yet one could hardly marry a man without meeting his family first. If nothing else, it was a simple matter of courtesy. Liam's approval or otherwise was surely by the way. It was Tris she was marrying, not the Oakleigh estate.

She went out alone for lunch, choosing a small but excellent restaurant a couple of streets away from the office, where she and Tristan were fairly well known. The proprietor greeted her with customary pleasantries regarding the spring weather, and himself showed her to their favourite table halfway down the narrow room, leaving her with the menu while he went back to despatch one of the waiters in her direction.

It was almost one-forty and the first rush of diners had been and gone. Several tables were already in the process of being relaid for late dinner that evening, the movement unobtrusive. It wasn't until Jaime had ordered and sat back with her tomato juice to await service that she spotted the couple at the table in the far corner, only fully visible through the mirror set at an angle on the wall beyond.

Her heart did a painful double thud before starting to beat again with surprising regularity as she gazed at the distinguished greying head bent towards the pale gold one belonging to his young companion. No doubt Gerald believed himself safe from observation in a place as relatively obscure as this. It was exactly the sort of restaurant he would have chosen to take her during those emotive few weeks of their acquaintance.

Two years ago, yet it could have been yesterday sitting here now watching that practised manner of his, the faint, wry smile on the fine patrician face, the possessive clasp of his hand over the smaller, slimmer one lying between them on the white cloth. Apart from the hair, that could so easily be herself sitting across from him, listening in wide-eyed adulation to the words which tripped so glibly off that silvered tongue. At twenty-two she had been old enough to know better than his present recipient, who couldn't be more than nineteen. Old enough, but certainly not sensible enough. She had gone overboard just as surely as this girl was in the process of doing right now.

Orphaned when she was sixteen, Jaime had spent the following couple of years living with her grandmother, until the death of that last of her surviving relatives had left her with her own living to make as best she might. The year she had just previously spent at business training college had stood her in good stead, together with a natural aptitude which advanced her rapidly through the various levels of office promotion until she had finally gained the much sought-after position of private secretary to the promotions director.

Gerald had been forty-six then, and devastating from the start. Inside a month he had so far undermined her girlish scruples as to persuade her that dinner with a married man in no way constituted a crime when said married man was so desperate for the understanding he failed to get from his wife. Before two months had passed they were seeing each other several times a week outside office hours, yet Jaime had managed to resist his urging to sleep with him. The invitation to accompany him on a weekend conference was something else again. Scared of losing his regard for her if she continued to put obstacles in the way of their achieving a complete relationship, she had agreed to go with him, telling herself that nothing else mattered but the fact that they loved each other.

Oddly enough, the conference had been held in Derbyshire too, she recalled now. A place called Ashbourne. She could see it in her mind's eye with its quaint old market square and buildings. Despite everything, it hadn't been until Gerald was signing them into the hotel under the same name that it had come home to her just what she was about to become. Mistress to a married man more than twice her age was not a title to be proud of. Watching the confident way in which he handled the situation, it had occurred to her to wonder for the first time if he had done this sort of thing before—a thought she had pushed hastily to the back of her mind because she didn't want to consider it.

Suspicion had hardly been allayed by the realisation at dinner that other delegates apart from Gerald were there with women quite obviously not their wives. Trying to act blasée about the whole affair, Jaime had drunk a little too much and laughed a great deal too much. At one point she had become aware of the cynical gaze of the man sitting a couple of tables away on his own. Even after two years she could recall those sardonic features in every detail—and feel the hot wave of shame that had swept over her under the knowing regard. Nevertheless, she had stuck it out until the moment when Gerald tried to take her in his arms after reaching their room, before finally breaking down and telling him she couldn't go through with it.

Somewhat predictably he had been furious, revealing a side to his nature she had hitherto not suspected in his final dismissal of her as a silly little kid fit only for the nursery. In the end, she had spent the night in an armchair while he occupied the double bed alone. First thing in the morning he had run her into Derby to catch the train for home, recovered a little from his previous night's rage but not by any means prepared to forgive and forget. She had known her job was finished along with their affair, and lived with the misery of that knowledge all the way back to London.

And here she was once more in love with her boss, she reflected now wryly. History repeating itself.

She caught herself up with a firm admonishment at that point. Of course it wasn't the same. How could it be? Tristan was not only unmarried but barely three years her senior to boot. Her feelings for him in no remote way resembled those she had known for Gerald, although at the time she had truly believed herself to be in love. Let the past stay in the past. It was where it belonged.

The couple were moving, preparing to leave. Jaime picked up the large menu still lying on the table and hid her face behind it as Gerald followed his young companion from the restaurant, breathing a sigh of relief when he was past and gone. She felt sorry for the girl, whoever she was—although perhaps her sympathies would be better reserved for his long-suffering wife, if he still had one.

Packing that evening didn't really take all that long. Finished tidying the small but pleasant flat by eight-thirty, Jaime half regretted telling Tris not to come round. She could have cooked a light meal for the two of them, and perhaps bought a bottle of wine. A quiet evening alone would have been nice, especially considering they were probably not going to have a great deal of time alone together once they reached Oakleigh.

She was in bed with the light out before trepidation finally caught up with her again. Silly to be so nervous of meeting this brother of Tristan's, she told herself. He might disapprove of the speed with which things had happened, but there was little he could do about it. Anyway, wasn't it up to her to make him accept her? She wasn't an outstandingly gregarious person, but she didn't usually have much trouble getting along with people. The best thing to do was to stop worrying and allow matters to take their course.

Tristan arrived promptly at nine. By ten they were heading north along the M1 in the comfort of his three-litre Capri.

'If you can wait till round one for lunch I can take you to a great little pub I know near Chesterfield,' he said at one point. He pulled a face. 'Better than anything we're likely to get along here.'

'Oh, I shan't be hungry for ages yet,' Jaime assured him. 'Are you sure they won't be expecting us at the house for lunch?'

'I told Liam mid-afternoon. No fun setting off at the crack of dawn—or getting in to sit straight down to a meal. This way we'll just have time to tidy up before tea.'

She gave him a smiling, sideways glance. 'Cucumber sandwiches?'

'With the crusts cut off,' he agreed with a return grin. 'Crumpets in winter. We do things properly at Oakleigh.'

'You must carry quite a staff.'

'Not enough. It isn't easy to get people these days. Hasn't been for a long time. I can remember my mother complaining about it when I was a boy.'

'Were you a well behaved little boy?' she asked. 'You must have looked angelic with that fair hair and blue eyes!'

'Looked, maybe, acted, definitely not. If there was trouble to get into you can bet I found it!' His tone was cheerful. 'Poor old Liam used to get it in the neck for not keeping a better eye on me. Not that you could blame him. Who wants an eight-year-old trailing round with you when you're going on seventeen and home from school for the hols? He had other interests in life.'

'You're not alike, then?'

'Not one iota. He's dark like Dad, while I favour Mother. Hard to know what he's thinking or feeling sometimes. He's always been a bit of a dark horse.'

'But obviously content to stay at home and run things.'

'I don't know about content. He does it because he's the eldest and inherited the responsibility. I was still at school when Dad died, so I was out of it. Anyway, he did his globe-trotting in his twenties, so he can hardly say he's been curtailed.'

Jaime lapsed into silence after that. The more she heard about Liam Caine the less she liked the sound of him, yet there was absolutely nothing Tris had said which gave her adequate reason for antagonism. She really must stop building on vague instincts. It was hardly fair to prejudge a man she knew so relatively little about.

They left the motorway at the Chesterfield exit, and drove through countryside scattered with signs of past mining activities. At one point there was a particularly obnoxious smell in the air which Tristan told her came from a large chemical plant at nearby Staveley.

'We're miles off Oakleigh yet,' he assured her. 'And it's green belt anyway. Any industry at all is on this side of the city, so don't start imagining factory chimneys belching out fumes where we're going. The nearest market town is Bakewell, and that's three miles away. Apart from the village we're pretty well isolated, although we do have good access to a main road.'

'Tris, you don't have to convince me,' Jaime said softly. 'I know Derbyshire is a beautiful county.'

His glance held surprise. 'You've been here before?'

'No.' The lie was out before she could stop it, stemming from an instinctive reaction. She bit her lip, disliking the deception yet aware of the explanations any retraction now would elicit. 'I've read about it, and seen photographs,' she tagged on truthfully. 'I remember it saying somewhere that there's a bit of almost every county in the country wrapped up in this one.'

'True enough,' he agreed. 'I could take you to spots where you'd swear you were in Kent or Devon, or even the west coast of Scotland. We'll have to try and get around a bit while we're here—although there'll be other times.' He slowed down and indicated right as a two-storied L-shaped building set at an angle to the roadway hove into view around a bend. 'Here we are. Doesn't look much from the outside, but wait till we get in.'

Jaime appreciated his meaning once inside the doors of what appeared to be the saloon bar. Oak beams and horse brasses gleamed with loving care. A huge log fire blazed in the stone fireplace, welcome in its warmth after the late April chill still lingering in the northern air. There were several tables ready set with cutlery and glassware towards the rear of the room. Tristan saw her seated at the only one still remaining vacant, and went to fetch copies of the menu from the bar.

Jaime chose rainbow trout offered at a price which would have had customers queuing up back home in London, and was further amazed to receive two whole fish along with all the trimmings on a large oval platter. She managed to get through them, but had to refuse a dessert, settling for coffee.

'Delicious,' she acknowledged when Tristan asked if she had enjoyed her meal. 'But I don't think I could get through a lunch like that every day of the week!'

'No, I'm a bit out of practice myself,' he confessed. 'Time was when I could have eaten that and another like it, and still gone on to pie and cream. We breed healthy appetites in the north!'

Jaime laughed. 'It must be something to do with the climate. This suit felt plenty warm enough when we left London, but I could have done with the heater on after we got north of Watford Gap.'

'Thin blood! You should have said.' Tristan lifted a casual hand to someone across the room, then glanced at his watch. 'Time we were making tracks. Only about half an hour from here, but I'd like to be home by three.'

After the snug warmth of the pub, the air outside felt chillier than ever. Tristan switched on the heater without being asked, smiling indulgently at her appreciative murmur.

'You'll soon harden off,' he said. 'And we do get warm days in summer.'

Jaime was too interested in the passing scenery to converse much during the following minutes. Coming to the bottom of the long steep hill from Chesterfield, they passed through a charming little village with a tri-cornered green and bow-windowed shops set about it. A half mile or so further on, they left the main road to bear left through a pair of huge iron gates into a rolling green park. Moments later, she was exclaiming in admiration at the sight of the great stately house so beautifully set amidst sculptured gardens against the background of wooded hills on the far side of a broad river.

'Chatsworth,' Tristan advised. 'The Duke of Devonshire's place. Dates back to the sixteenth century, although various Dukes have rebuilt most of it. It's superb inside.'

Jaime blinked. 'You go *visiting*?'

The laugh came easily. 'We're hardly in *that* league. It's open to visitors. That's what all the cars are doing here. Oakleigh would fit into one wing of that place—and we don't do conducted tours.'

Didn't need to, Jaime surmised. Better to be small and viable than great and deadweight. She was thankful Oakleigh wasn't like this. Stately houses were okay for the stately people, but they were in no way homely.

As an adjective the latter word did scant justice to her first sight of her future home. They approached it from the south-west, crunching up a long, gravelled, tree-lined drive to draw to a sweeping halt before the square, ivy-covered bulk. Long sash windows gleamed in the afternoon sunlight, as also did the great oak door varnished against the elements.

'Welcome to the Caine residence,' said Tristan, coming round the car to open the door for her. 'Think I ought to carry you over the threshold?'

'Not this time round.' Jaime was laughing as she put out her hands to fend him off. 'Tris, behave yourself!'

The front door opened suddenly and a man appeared on the stone step within the archway created by the columns flanking the entrance. He was wearing casual tweed slacks and a light sweater. Meeting the cynical gaze over Tristan's shoulder, Jaime felt the laughter die, the breath catch sharply and painfully in her throat.

'Don't stand about outside, Tris,' he said shortly. 'Bring your fiancée indoors.'

Tristan took Jaime's hand firmly in his and drew her forward with him. 'Meet big brother Liam. His bark's worse than his bite.'

'Depends,' returned the older man with a faint twist of of his lips. Grey eyes suddenly narrowed as they rested on Jaime's face, the expression in them undergoing a change. The hand he had extended was firm in its grasp; it could have been her imagination that those lean, hard fingers tautened still further for a fraction of a second before letting hers go.

Somehow she found herself ushered ahead of him into a broad hallway floored in polished oak. A staircase curved gracefully up from the centre to a galleried landing. A middle-aged woman with a plain but kindly face came out through a door towards the rear to greet Tristan with obvious pleasure, the latter emotion fading a little as he turned to introduce Jaime.

'This is Mrs Paxton, our household treasure,' he said. 'She keeps the whole place running like clockwork!'

'Not always when you're around, Mr Tristan,' came the dry reply. 'Although it's been long enough since you were here last.'

'I know. Time flies.' His tone was repentant. 'Are we having some of your balm cake for tea?'

'I'll think about it.'

'Jaime might like to see her room before tea,' Liam suggested. 'Tris will bring up your luggage when he fetches it in from the car.'

She murmured a word of agreement, and followed the housekeeper up the staircase in the certain knowledge that those grey eyes were still on her.

The room she was to occupy was towards the rear of the house, overlooking broad lawns and a long terrace. It was large, and beautifully furnished in the seemingly inevitable oak, with a fine woven carpet in beige and cream on the floor. The bed was a double, and looked comfortable beneath the silk cover which matched the apricot drapes.

Mrs Paxton showed her the adjoining bathroom, and waved an admonishing finger at Tris as he hefted in Jaime's suitcase and made to hoist it on to the bed.

'You know better than that, Mr Tristan. It goes on the stand there!'

Tris grinned and winked at Jaime as the woman left them. 'Now I know I'm home!'

'How long has she been with you?' Jaime asked diffidently.

'Pax? Oh, years! She came after Mother died when I was fifteen.'

'What about Mr Paxton?'

'There isn't one. She's been a widow all the time we've known her. Expect she'll stay one now. Tea's at four. Will you come down on your own, or shall I call for you?'

'I'll come down on my own.' She put distance between them by moving across to where he had parked her suitcase. 'I'll just have time to do a quick change if I hurry.'

Tristan took the hint. 'I'll leave you to it then. See you in half an hour.'

Alone at last, Jaime sank down on the immaculate bedcover to stare at the closed door with unseeing eyes as she tried to pull her thoughts together. How cruel could fate be to cross her path with this man of all men again! It had been apparent that he recognised her from somewhere, but whether or not he remembered the actual circumstances still remained open to doubt.

Strange how his face had stayed so clear in her memory these last two years. She could see him now sitting at the adjoining table in the hotel in Ashbourne, strong mouth curling a little as he caught her eye. If he did remember, what did she say to him? What *could* she say? She was caught fairly and squarely in a web of circumstances no amount of explanation could untangle.

CHAPTER TWO

THE brothers were together in the fine drawing room when Jaime went downstairs again. A log fire burned brightly in the Adam-styled fireplace despite the central heating radiators placed unobtrusively about the room. She thought the latter most probably turned off now that spring was here.

The furnishings were in walnut, pleasing to her eye in their graceful lines and indicative of a woman's touch. The deep club chairs and chesterfield covered in plain gold rep looked comfortable and essentially masculine—an addition in latter years, perhaps.

Jaime had changed into a fine wool dress in an amber colour which brought out the highlights in her hair, conscious of the need to face the coming moments with all the confidence she could muster. Tristan greeted her with an approving smile.

'Come and have some tea. We've been waiting for you to do the honours.'

She laughed, not trusting herself to glance his brother's way. 'Who usually does them?'

'No one,' said Liam. 'If I'm in the house at all this time of day I usually have it in the kitchen.'

'Time we regained some civilised habits,' Tris put in cheerfully. 'Mother would have died a thousand deaths! There were only two ways of doing anything according to her—the right way and the wrong way!'

'She was raised in a time where it mattered,' the other came back on a mild note. 'Standards change.' He took his cup from Jaime with a word of thanks and added casually, 'Did you ever visit Derbyshire before?'

The question could have meant everything or nothing. Considering her reply to the same one from Tristan earlier, there was only one thing she could say, busying herself with the silver teapot as she did so. 'No, I haven't. I'm looking forward to seeing more of it.' She gave Tristan his cup and hastily changed the subject. 'This is a beautiful house. Were all the furnishings originally oak?'

It was Liam who answered. 'It was my grandfather's idea to make the name fit throughout—one he rather overdid in some respects.'

'Mother refurnished the downstairs rooms soon after she arrived,' Tristan said. 'The name itself came from the stand of oak trees on the north side of the house. We're very proud of those. They date back over two hundred years.'

'You'll have to give Jaime a conducted tour,' came the dry comment.

'A la Chatsworth?' He grinned. 'I brought her in via the park. She asked if we were on visiting terms with the Duke.'

There was irony in the grey glance. 'Would you like to be on visiting terms with a duke?'

'Not unless I could practise my curtsy first,' Jaime said lightly. 'I understand you breed horses?'

'That's right. Want me to find you a suitable mount while you're here?'

'I'm afraid I don't ride.' She tried to make it a statement rather than an apology, and felt she didn't fully succeed. 'To be quite honest, I've never even sat on a horse.'

'What an admission!' Tris was laughing. 'In this

family everybody rides! Liam will teach you. He's more patience than I have.'

Jaime doubted it. That mouth of his brother's suggested anything but tolerance. A man of strong passions, she found herself thinking, sneaking a surreptitious glance at the firmly cut profile. A man who knew what he wanted and went out after it: not a man to cross if one could help it. She hoped she wouldn't have to.

'I'll hardly be here long enough this time for any proper tuition,' she responded. 'I imagine it takes longer than a few days to scrape an acquaintance with what it's all about.'

Liam's shrug was easy. 'You could be right. Let's see how things go. I've invited the Morrisons over for dinner tomorrow night, Tris.'

A shadow seemed to cross Tristan's face for a moment, but his voice sounded normal enough. 'Be nice to see them again.' To Jaime he added, 'They're our closest neighbours, and old friends. Michael and Liam went through university together. You'll like Libby, Michael's wife. She's a foreigner too—all the way from Sheffield!'

'Which is where I've got to go right now.' Liam drained his cup and put it down. 'See you both at dinner, if not before.'

Jaime looked expectantly at Tristan as the door closed behind his brother, but he was staring into his cup as though he expected to find something written in the tea-leaves, a certain bleakness about his normally insouciant countenance.

'Want to show me round the house, Tris?' she asked.

'What?' His head came up, expression blank for a moment before he realised what she had said. 'Oh, yes, sure.' The familiar smile came back. 'Guides require tipping, though.'

The tour took quite some time. There were eight bedrooms, four of them with bathrooms now incorporated, in addition to a whole range of attics containing a fascinating collection of stored jumble.

'These used to be the servants' quarters in the days when the whole staff used to live in,' Tristan told her. 'In my mother's day they became a place to store all the things she couldn't bear to throw away.' A smile on his lips, he gently rocked the large wooden horse minus most of its mane and bearing the scars of enthusiastic usage along its painted sides and neck. 'Old Brutus here saw Dad through as well as Liam and me. They don't make things to last any more.'

Jaime thought he might go on to say he would have it done up for the children they would one day have, but he didn't. His mind seemed oddly detached from what they were doing. She wanted to ask him if anything were wrong, but something stopped her. He was probably just tired from the journey, she reasoned. She felt it too, and she had only been a passenger.

Downstairs again, he showed her the sitting room with its french windows opening on to the terrace, taking her along the latter and back inside the house via the dining room next door, where the oak refectory table and leather-upholstered chairs held pride of place in the centre of a magnificent Aubusson carpet. There was a fireplace in here too, built of stone this time, with an iron grate shaped like a casket on sturdy feet.

The study came last, book-lined and wood-panelled, one wall lined with rosettes and other evidence of horsemanship. Rather more Liam than Tris, Jaime acknowledged when he sat down for a moment at the huge desk set at right angles to the window. The latter looked more at home in a modern setting geared towards maximum efficiency. At five feet ten he didn't have quite the stature to take on this room.

'That's it,' he said now. 'Apart from the kitchen, of course, and Pax's little flatlet at the back. She's the only living-in staff we carry. There's a couple of women come in daily from the village to clean the place, and a girl who acts as general maid when we have people in. Pax does all the cooking. She's a wonder. We're darn lucky to have her!'

'I suppose she might feel herself just as lucky to have a position like this one where she's regarded as almost one of the family,' Jaime ventured.

'Oh, she is one of the family, make no mistake. Oakleigh couldn't carry on without her. Whoever becomes mistress here first, Liam's wife or mine, she's going to have to be prepared to share the responsibility for running the place to a certain extent.'

Something about that statement bothered Jaime a little. Nothing she could put her finger on; more a feeling.

'Liam is thinking of getting married, then?' she asked.

'Not that I know of, but it could happen. It nearly did a few years ago, as a matter of fact.'

'He changed his mind?'

'No, she did. She married someone else. Oakleigh was too confining for a woman of Lillian's temperament.' He stirred restlessly. 'Want to see outside now?'

Jaime shook her head. 'Let's leave that till morning. I think I'll finish my unpacking.'

'Okay, fine.'

He got up and came back round the desk, reaching for her to kiss her with an intensity that surprised her. Whether he found what he was looking for in her response she had no way of knowing, for there was nothing to read in his face when he drew back.

'See you later,' was all he said.

In her room again, she tried to tell herself she was imagining the subtle change that had come over Tris in the last couple of hours. She was being over-sensitive, reading something into nothing. It was perhaps that his brother had a somewhat chastening effect on him, although nothing Liam had said or done so far had struck her that way. Of the two, he was the stronger character, though, as well as being the elder. That alone could be enough.

She heard the car return at six-thirty. At seven, dressed in a plain green velvet skirt and black top, she made her way downstairs, uncertain as to what time they might be eating. The drawing room was empty, the fire almost dead. She found one lit instead in the smaller sitting room across the hall, and sat down in front of it in a wing chair which almost hid her from view.

There was the sound of movement from the dining room next door, a dull thud as though a cupboard door had been closed. If the table was only just being set, she was probably far too early. Not that it mattered, providing Tris came down first. Facing Liam again at all would be unnerving enough without doing it alone. If only she could be certain that his memory would not supply the answer to that momentary recognition! He seemed to have put the matter out of mind, but she couldn't be all that sure.

To her relief the brothers came in together. Liam greeted her pleasantly enough, allaying her fears still further. Like Tristan, he wore a suit, which seemed to bely his statement that standards no longer mattered to him all that much.

Tris himself appeared to have regained his normal equilibrium. He came to sit on the arm of Jaime's chair, dropping a light kiss on the top of her head.

'Hi,' he said softly. 'Still love me?'

She smiled up at him, aware of Liam's cynical regard on them through the mirror which hung over the table where he was pouring drinks. 'Of course.'

Liam brought their glasses across, went back for his own and lifted it towards them in a gesture Jaime found somewhat less than enthusiastic. 'Good luck,' he said.

They ate at eight, helping themselves from the serving dishes Mrs Paxton brought in and left on the table. Jaime felt herself relaxing under the soothing influence of the wine Liam produced to go with the main course. the tension draining from her. It was going to be all right. If he had been going to remember at all he would have done so by now. She hated the necessity to deceive, yet it was so obviously necessary. She hadn't told Tris about Gerald because she was basically ashamed of the episode, and now it was too late. Confession was often merely a self-indulgence anyway, she reminded herself: a clearing of conscience at the cost of another's peace of mind. Let it pass.

Unwittingly, it was Tris himself who brought about her downfall. They were nearing the end of the meal when he started talking about business matters, asking Liam how things were going with plans for expansion.

'We've three bulk purchase units already established,' Liam told him. 'Customers phone through their order and we deliver to the nearest within forty-eight hours, pre-packed ready for the freezer. Ashbourne's next on the list. I'm due over there Tuesday week to get things started. Probably take a couple of days to sort out the details. I remember what it was like trying to get the shop converted when we first opened up there a couple of years back. I spent long enough on the spot to have done the job myself!'

Jaime had frozen the moment he had mentioned Ashbourne. Fatalistically now, she registered the sudden abruptness with which he stopped speaking, saw the swift change of expression in his eyes as they swung in her direction. No doubting the recognition in them this time; he *knew*. She returned his gaze with what equanimity she could muster, and was only too well aware of her failure to deceive. He not only remembered, but knew that she remembered too. And the reckoning was yet to come.

How she got through the rest of that interminable evening she never knew. Tristan seemed to be unaware of any change in the atmosphere, although to Jaime his brother's coldness was too obvious to be missed. She was half relieved, half apprehensive when the time came to retire for the night. If Liam didn't intend saying anything in front of Tris, when was he waiting for?

Parting at the door of her room, Tristan said lightly, 'Don't expect to see me around before nine in the morning. I'm not an early riser. If you get down before me you can go and have a look at the stables with Liam. A word of warning—don't pretend to understand what he's talking about if you don't. There's nothing drives him up the wall quicker than a show of pseudo-interest.'

'Most people would rather make an effort to pretend interest than show they're actually bored to death,' Jaime returned with some asperity. 'But I'll make a note to remember his preferences.'

Tristan studied her for a moment, mouth rueful. 'You don't like him very much, do you?'

'I don't know him.' Jaime had a feeling that was a matter to be rectified in the not too distant future, though when was anybody's guess. She summoned a smile. 'I daresay I'll learn.'

She was to do so sooner than she had anticipated. On the point of switching out the bedside lamp some twenty minutes later, she was halted by a soft but decisive rap on the door. She knew who it was, of course. She just hadn't expected him to come to her room at this time of night.

For a moment she contemplated ignoring it, pretending to be asleep, but apparently Liam was not the kind to be put off by minor details, for the knock came again, a little louder this time. Jaime bit her lip and pushed back the bedcovers, reaching for the silky blue wrap she had just taken off. She might as well get it over with, she supposed.

He was still fully dressed, one hand resting on the door jamb so that he seemed to tower threateningly close when she opened the door. His mouth was unsmiling.

'This isn't a social call,' he said. 'What we have to discuss isn't going to be pleasant.'

Even then instinct made her try to bluff it out. 'I can't think of anything we might have to discuss. Especially at this time of night. Surely ...'

'You know what I'm getting at.' He came into the room, forcing her to step back, closing the door behind him to lean against it with a look which said more plainly than words that she wasn't going to escape him. 'You recognised me immediately when you saw me on the step this afternoon. I was pretty sure I'd seen you before too, but I told myself it was just a chance resemblance to someone I know. It wasn't until a couple of hours ago when Tris was talking about the business that I remembered where and when I'd seen you.' His glance was assessing, moving down over her slender shape with deliberation. 'I must say, you no more look the type now than you did then. Under any other circumstances I'd be ready to swear you were everything Tris apparently thinks you are.'

Her head came up. There was small point in denying it further. 'What makes you so sure I haven't told him the whole story?'

'Because I know Tris, and he wouldn't wear it. He might be prepared to accept a previous love affair with a man round your own age, but definitely not the kind of sordid arrangement you had at twenty-two with a man old enough to be your father!' There was contempt in the last. 'I'd have said that was your first time. How many more have there been since?'

Jaime flushed, said thickly, 'That was uncalled for!'

'I don't think so. Girls that age usually only go with older men for what they can get out of them, and having tasted good living don't want to give it up. Tris was a lucky find, wasn't he? You certainly wasted no time in hooking him!'

'I didn't set out to hook him. I was as surprised as anyone when he asked me to marry him.' Her voice caught a little. 'I'm beginning to realise now that I should have waited for his brother's go-ahead!'

'But you were so much in love with him you couldn't wait to say yes.' It was a calculated sneer.

Jaime said quietly, 'I do love him, yes. Very much. He's a very lovable person.'

'And an excellent catch.' He continued to lean against the door regarding her with cynical eyes. 'I suppose you'll say next that you'd have felt just the same about him if he'd been a struggling clerk.'

'Oh, stop it,' she burst out. 'That's a stupid question! How do I know how I'd have felt? Born into a different environment, he might not even have been the same kind of person.'

'Very glib,' he said admiringly. 'I understand both your parents are dead?'

'Yes, they are.' Anger and resentment sparkled in her eyes. 'But you don't have to worry about them. They were perfectly respectable!'

'Oh, I'm not worrying. Not about anything.' His tone was deceptively quiet. 'Before this week is out I want this engagement broken off—either by you yourself or by Tris.'

She stared at him for a long moment, searching the hard-hewn features in growing dismay. 'You can't mean that,' she whispered at last. 'You haven't even given me a chance to explain about Gerald. I ...'

'Spare me the details,' he cut in. 'It's a story I've heard many times before. You knew what you were doing that time. You even had the grace to look embarrassed when you realised you weren't deceiving anybody with that married act! But not enough, it seems, to change your mind. I had a room on the same stretch of landing. I saw the two of you go into yours.'

'I'm not denying that part.' Her voice was low and pain-filled. 'We shared a room that night, yes, but I didn't ... I couldn't ...'

Dark brows lifted sardonically. 'You're trying to tell me you didn't sleep with him, is that it? Don't take me for a fool!'

'That would be the last thing I'd take you for,' she came back between clenched teeth. 'But a narrow-minded bigot wouldn't be too short of the mark. It wouldn't matter what I told you, you'd only believe what you want to! Well, go ahead and think what you like. I don't care about *your* opinion!'

'You care about Tristan's, though. At least, so far as it affects your relationship.' The attack had left him unmoved. 'You can have the choice. Either you tell him, or I will.'

'All right.' Jaime's face was pale but her head was held high. 'I'll tell him. I'm not going to pretend he'll like it, but he'll at least let me tell him the whole story—and believe me.'

'If you really thought that you'd have risked it before this.' Liam paused as if considering, came to some apparent decision and added hardily, 'There's maybe something else you should know. About two years ago, Tris was engaged to Michael Morrison's younger sister. They'd have been married by now, except that they had a row and Susan went storming off to visit relatives in South Africa.'

In the following sentence, Jaime could only think painfully that Tris had had his secrets too. The news had shaken her; she had to force herself to meet the watchful grey eyes without letting the depths of her sudden uncertainty show through.

'Perhaps it was as well they found out before rather than after that they weren't suited.'

'I didn't say they weren't suited, I said they had a row. One of those relatively minor things that blows up out of all proportion.'

'In your opinion, perhaps.'

'In everyone's opinion—including Tris himself.'

Her breath caught. 'Then why hasn't he done anything about making things up?'

'Pride, purely and simply. They each wanted the other to be the one to say they were wrong.'

It was pride which kept Jaime going right at that moment. 'All the same, if he still felt anything for her he wouldn't have asked me to marry him, would he?'

'Wouldn't he?' he asked softly. 'Not even if I tell you how like her you look? That colouring of yours is distinctive, and not exactly common. Odd he should pick it out again. You're about the same height, the same build —even the same basic temperament.'

Jaime said huskily, 'You don't know anything about my temperament.'

'I can make a fair guess. Deceptively quiet and well balanced until something happens to upset your applecart, then look out for sparks!' His tone held irony. 'Right?'

'You've forgotten my avaricious streak. Is *that* something we share too?'

His upper lip curled. 'Don't confuse the issue. You're talking about character now. Hers I can vouch for. Yours ...' He paused and shrugged. 'It speaks for itself.'

'Only in your mind.' She was trembling with the need to stop herself from lashing out at him. 'What's the point in going into all this anyway? If she's in South Africa she ...'

'She isn't.' He said it so calmly it took a moment to sink in. 'She arrived home a couple of days after Tris phoned to tell me about you. Coincidental, wasn't it? None of us knew she was coming until she arrived. Apparently it had to be like that or she'd never have done it at all. So far as anybody was aware, she planned on staying over there for good.' He paused briefly. 'It was the worst kind of homecoming present I had to give her.'

'I can imagine.' Jaime was trying hard to put herself in the other girl's shoes for a moment or two. 'And I really do sympathise with her. But you're wrong about Tris. I know you are!'

'You mean you want to believe I am.' He had straightened away from the door and was standing with hand thrust into trouser pockets, the hardness still there in his features. 'You saw the way he reacted this afternoon when I mentioned the Morrisons by name. She still means something to him—just how much we'll find out tomorrow night when they come over.'

'You're going to spring her on him without telling him first?' Jaime's voice was barely audible.

'That's the general idea. He needs a shock to make him see what a fool he's been. And in case you're thinking of warning him, the degree of shock would be even worse coming from you, and won't make the slightest difference to his actual reaction.'

It was grasping at straws, but she had to have something to hang on to. 'Supposing you're wrong,' she managed. 'Supposing he no longer wants Susan? Would you still insist on his knowing about me?'

He looked at her for what seemed an age before answering, an unreadable expression in his eyes.

'I'll strike a bargain with you,' he said unexpectedly at last. 'If Tris shows nothing at all towards Susan I won't contradict your version of the affair—providing you do tell him.'

'Why?' she said. 'Why hurt him any more than he's already been hurt in the past?'

'He has a right to know.'

'No more than I had a right to know about his previous engagement.'

'It's hardly the same thing. Theirs was a love match.'

'So was mine.' Her tone was embittered. 'At least, I thought it was at the time. Didn't you ever make a mistake?'

'I've made my share,' he came back indifferently. 'It isn't me we're discussing.'

'Tris is as capable as you are of looking after his own interests.'

'No, he isn't. He never has been. Tris was always impulsive. He does things off the top without stopping to consider the consequences.' Liam shook his head. 'I can't stop him marrying you if he has his heart set on it, but I can and will make sure he knows he isn't the first!'

'Swine!' she choked.

'That's right.' He had a hand on the doorknob. 'I've met glib-tongued little fortune-hunters like you before.'

The retort came short and sharp. 'Did she throw you over for someone even richer?'

Twin fires blazed suddenly in the grey eyes. He let go of the doorknob and reached her in a couple of strides, hands merciless as they pulled her towards him, lips parting hers in a kiss which took her breath along with every ounce of fight left in her. She was off balance when he finally pushed her away from him, and had to put out a hand to the back of the nearby chair for support. Nothing in her experience had ever prepared her for anger of that intensity.

Liam was breathing hard, contempt in his face. 'Don't tempt providence,' he said. 'I'd hate to disillusion Tris totally where you're concerned.'

Jaime remained where she was for several moments after the door had closed behind him. She felt bruised all over, mentally as well as physically. So she had hit a raw spot, she thought painfully. She knew what that felt like. Men were at a distinct advantage when it came to retaliation, though. They could make a woman feel cheap in one contemptuous gesture. What way did she have of getting back at him?

The night was long and hardly restful. Jaime rose at six-thirty, unable to bear the inactivity any longer. At present there were two choices open to her. She could ask Tristan now, this morning, about Susan, and put herself out of at least some of her misery, or she could do as Liam had said and wait until this evening when the other girl would be putting in an appearance. Neither way appealed, the former least of all because it called for immediate decision on her part. Coward! she told herself wryly, but it made little difference.

She hung around her room after nine, unable to bring herself to run the risk of finding Liam alone at the breakfast table on this bright and sunny day. The knock on the door just as she was about ready to go brought a jerking of nerve and sinew quickly relieved by the sound of Tristan's voice.

'Hey, sleepyhead! It's gone nine!'

Jaime went to open the door, seeing his laughing face with a sense of release from the night's haunting fears. Liam was wrong. He had to be wrong. Tris couldn't look as lighthearted as this if he were secretly pining for another girl!

'I waited for you,' she said. 'I've been up for ages.'

'Tell that to the Marines. You just don't like admitting you overslept! And here I am forcing an unwilling body out at some unnatural hour purely on your behalf.' His kiss matched his tone, tender and teasing. 'Come on down and eat before Pax starts clearing away.'

On the way downstairs he said, 'I thought we might take the car and see some of the local sights today, while the weather holds. Pub lunch again, if you like. We've dozens to choose from.'

'I'd like that,' Jaime agreed, and meant it, not least for the reason that she would be out of Liam's way for the day.

To her relief the dining room was empty. Tris had

already eaten, but he sat with her while she breakfasted on toast and marmalade and black coffee from the fresh pot Mrs Paxton brought dourly in.

'She disapproves of timid appetites,' he said with a grin when the housekeeper had departed. 'You might have gone up a couple of notches in her estimation if you'd asked for ham and eggs!'

Jaime said lightly, 'I suppose I'm considered a foreigner coming from the south.'

'Oh, don't think the girls up here are any different. The buxom country lass image went out with plus-fours for men.'

'You're too young to remember plus-fours.'

'Only just. My father had some he still wore for shooting.' He fidgeted a little, obviously impatient to be on the move. 'Nearly finished?'

Jaime had, but couldn't resist the urge to tease. 'Perhaps I should go and change into something more suitable.'

'I can't think of anything more suitable than slacks and a sweater,' he assured her. 'Why do women always have to be changing all the time?' He saw her smile then, and grinned. 'Wretched wench! You're having me on!'

They got away from the house without seeing any sign of Liam. Only then did Jaime fully relax, closing her mind to thoughts of the evening. Liam only thought he knew his brother so well; it didn't have to follow he was right. There was nothing in Tris this morning to suggest his love lay anywhere but with her. As to the rest—well, she refused to let that worry her at present either. If the time came that she had to confess her sins he would understand. That was what love was all about.

CHAPTER THREE

IT was an enjoyable day in every way. Tristan drove her, as he afterwards put it, halfway round the county. Only once was that enjoyment marred a little for Jaime on recognising the market town through which they were passing at the time. She barely registered what Tris was saying as they motored past the hotel where she had stayed with Gerald that fateful night, thankful he had not suggested stopping there. Not that it would make any difference if Liam had his way.

So why not tell him now and get it over with? a small inner voice prompted sensibly. Jaime tried, but the words stuck in her throat. It was no use, she acknowledged. She had to find the right time and place. Whether they would present themselves or have to be manufactured there was no way of telling; it was a chance she had to take.

They got back to Oakleigh at six, tired but happy. Liam was crossing the hall towards the study when they went in. He paused when he saw them, face expressionless.

'Had a good day?' he asked.

'Great!' Tristan answered. 'We've been places I haven't seen for years. Right down to Uttoxeter.'

The grey glance shifted fleetingly to Jaime. 'Through Ashbourne?'

'We came back that way, stopping off in Dove Dale at that cottage café for tea.' Tris flexed his shoulders and grimaced. 'Amazing what sitting in a car can do when you're not used to long stretches. I feel as stiff as a board!'

'You haven't forgotten the Morrisons are coming tonight?' his brother asked, and gained a reaction in the faint jerk of the other head.

'No, I haven't forgotten. What time?'

'I told them round about seven-thirty so we could catch up on general news before dinner. Must be five or six weeks since I saw them myself.' Liam's tone was lacking in any kind of underlying emphasis. 'See you both later.'

Jaime took her leave of Tris at the top of the stairs and went to her room. The doubts were back in full force despite all she could do to reassure herself that they were groundless. There was no mistaking the fact that even the name Morrison struck a chord in Tristan's emotions.

Yet wouldn't it do that anyway if he had once been in love with one of the family? It was difficult enough not to feel jealous of that former love without making things worse by believing Liam's theory that it might still exist. Tris had asked *her* to marry him, therefore it must follow that he loved her now. She had to convince herself of that.

She chose a long skirted kaftan in mid-brown edged at the neckline and sleeves with gold braid for the evening. Her only jewellery apart from her engagement ring was an intricately worked gold bracelet which had been her mother's. It was necessary to apply a little more makeup than she was accustomed to using in order to mask a certain lack of colour in her cheeks. Vanity, or sheer bravado? she found herself wondering.

She heard the visitors arrive at seven-forty, and gave them a few minutes before going down, reluctant to be there when Tristan first set eyes on the girl who had gone away and left him. By ten minutes to the hour, she knew she could credibly delay no longer, and left the room with fast beating heart and a prayer at the back of her mind.

Coming out on to the galleried landing, she could hear voices coming from the drawing room below. She paused for a moment to gather her resources before descending to meet the visitors, and was suddenly riveted to the spot by the words which came floating up the well of the staircase immediately below her.

'I came back to say I was sorry, Tris.' The girl's voice had a catch in it. 'I ought to have known it would be too late.'

'I thought you were never coming back.' He sounded ragged. 'It's been nearly two years, Susan. Two years, and not even a letter!'

'You didn't write either. I waited and waited!' There was a pause; Jaime could almost sense the wry smile. 'Liam always said we're both too pigheaded for our own good. He was right, wasn't he? If we hadn't been such a pair of fools we could have straightened things out.'

'Oh, God, Susan!' The wretchedness in his voice was a blow to Jaime's heart. 'What can I say?'

'Nothing. Liam should have told you I was home.'

'I know why he didn't. He wanted to make me realise ...' He broke off abruptly. 'I'd better go and see what's keeping Jaime.'

Mobility returned to Jaime's limbs by sheer force of will, turning her round and carrying her swiftly back to her room. When Tristan appeared round the angle of the landing, she appeared to be in the act of emerging.

'Sorry I took so long,' she said, and was surprised at the steadiness of her voice. 'I lost track of the time.'

'It doesn't matter,' He made a visible effort to put on his usual lighthearted smile. 'You look lovely. Come and meet everybody.' The pause was brief but telling. 'We're one more than we thought. Michael's sister is home unexpectedly from South Africa.'

Jaime was thankful he made no attempt to touch her as they descended the stairs side by side. She didn't think she could have borne that. Her mind felt numb, along with her emotions. She moved like an automaton, obeying an impulse which told her to keep the pretence going at all costs until there was time to think.

At first impression the drawing room seemed full of people despite its size. Liam was nearest to the door, back half turned as he bent his arrogant dark head towards an attractive woman in blue. A step beyond her stood a thin-featured man with reddish hair about Liam's own age who had to be Michael Morrison. Susan stood on her own to one side, eyes on the door with a look of numbed anticipation Jaime found echoed in her own heart.

She managed to make the appropriate responses when introduced to Elizabeth and Michael, but could summon no more than a smile and a faint 'Hallo' for Susan herself. She sensed Liam's regard but in no way could bring herself to face the mockery she knew would be in his eyes. She wouldn't put it past him to have engineered that confrontation in the hall in the hope that she would see the two of them together. He was certainly only too well aware of the change in his brother's demeanour since having the fateful surprise sprung upon him.

It took Libby Morrison to put the obvious into words. 'You know, you two could almost be sisters,' she remarked brightly. 'If Sue's hair was longer the resemblance would be quite startling. Such an unusual shade too!'

The atmosphere grew as the evening progressed. Only

Liam seemed immune to discomfiture. He was the perfect host, keeping the glasses filled, the small talk going, presiding over the dinner table with an ease that signified no need of any woman in his life.

Tristan did his best to act like a man with something to celebrate. but it was an attempt doomed to failure from the start and Jaime was not the only one aware of it. He was a man impaled on the horns of a dilemma, and suffering because of it. In spite of her own heartache, Jaime could only feel sorry for him. Liam should have warned him about Susan's return, given him an opportunity to sort out his emotions in private. This way was painful for everyone.

Coffee was served through in the sitting room before another of the cosy log fires.

'Pity it's still too cold to eat out on the terrace,' Libby remarked to nobody in particular. 'It's been a long winter this year. I only hope we get a good summer to make up for it. Have you named the new colt yet, Liam?'

He shook his head. 'I didn't want to tempt providence.'

'It would hardly be doing that now. He seems fine.' She glanced towards Jaime sitting beside a silent Tristan on the sofa, adding for the stranger's benefit, 'Liam's top brood mare dropped her foal three weeks early. It was touch and go for a time, but he's a real dandy now. You haven't seen the stables yet?'

'I'll take you round in the morning,' Liam put in before she had chance to answer, and got to his feet. 'Have another brandy, Mike.'

The Morrisons left at eleven-thirty. Susan had barely uttered a word all evening and looked as if she were being rent in two when she said goodnight to Tris. There was mute appeal in the dark brown eyes which briefly met Jaime's before she accompanied her brother and his wife out to the waiting car, as if she perhaps recognised some underlying sympathy.

'Nightcap?' Liam suggested, closing the outer door when the car had departed. His manner was easy, ignoring the tension still prevalent in the air.

Tris shook his head, avoiding Jaime's eyes. 'I think I'll go straight up. Too much driving this last couple of days. I feel shattered.'

Jaime surprised herself right then. 'You do,' she said, and even managed a smile of sorts. 'I'll keep your brother company.'

She was moving as she spoke, unable to bear the thought of his goodnight kiss with Liam looking on. The pain was there inside her, yet somehow apart from her too, leaving her cold and bitter with anger. Liam had a lot to answer for.

He followed her into the sitting room and closed the door softly, standing there for a moment looking across at her before moving towards the drinks tray.

'I don't want anything.' Her voice sounded thin and too high-pitched; she made an effort to control it. 'All right, so you sprang your little surprise. What do you think you've proved?'

He turned, glass in hand, but stayed where he was. 'I'd think that was obvious.'

'It was obvious that Tris had a shock seeing Susan again after all this time without any warning. It could hardly be anything else!'

'And that's all you saw?' His tone held irony. 'None so blind as those who don't want to see! Tris wasn't just surprised, he was thrown. He's been a fool and he knows it. He's still in love with Susan.'

'You can't be sure of that,' she came back desperately. 'Tris himself is the only one who can decide how he feels about anything. Did you really believe I'd just opt out without even giving him a chance to do that?'

Liam shrugged broad shoulders. 'If the thought crossed my mind I should have known better. You're hardly the type to make that kind of sacrifice.' The pause was brief, his glance calculating. 'I could be persuaded to make it worth your while.'

Jaime went white and then flushed hotly as the blood surged in her veins. 'That's just the sort of thing I might have expected from you,' she said. 'Do you judge everyone by your own standards? I don't want your money! I don't want anything *you* can give me, only ... only ...' to her dismay she felt the tears spring in her eyes and could do nothing to stop them overflowing. She turned hastily away from his regard, voice muffled and thick. 'I'm not what you think I am, Liam. I love your brother, not his position in life or what he might be able to give me. Why do you have to be such a cynic about everyone and everything!'

It seemed a long time before there was any response to the impassioned plea. Then she heard him move, felt him at her back and saw his hand extended out of the corner of her blurred vision holding a clean handkerchief.

'Use it,' he said. 'I'll get you that drink.'

Jaime obeyed, despising herself for a weak little fool, yet unable to stiffen her backbone enough to tell him what to do with both his handkerchief and his drink. When he came back with the glass she took it without looking at him.

'Brandy,' he said. His tone sounded different, not exactly gentle but certainly lacking in some of its former hostility. 'Sit down, Jaime.'

When she shook her head he took her by the arm and moved her firmly across to a chair, putting her into it and standing back a little to view her with a certain wryness about the line of his mouth.

'All right,' he said, 'so maybe I'm wrong about you. Maybe you really do have some feeling for Tris.' He saw the jerk of her chin and held up a hand. 'I know, there's no maybe about it where you're concerned, but you have to admit there's room for doubt on my side.'

'Because of something that happened two years ago?'

'Not entirely. The whole thing happened too fast, that's all. You've only worked for Lockharts a few weeks. That's hardly time for two people to get to know one another, much less engaged.'

She looked up at him for the first time in minutes, registering the indecision in his eyes. 'It doesn't have to take months or years to be sure of the way you feel about someone. I didn't chase after Tris. It didn't even occur to me that he might be interested until the day he asked me out to dinner. We just seemed to get on so well, that's all. Right from that very first time. We work well together too.'

'Do you sleep with him?' The question came bluntly.

Jaime flushed again but answered with relative calm. 'That's something you don't have any right to ask, but as it happens I don't!'

'Because he hasn't asked you, or because you refused?'

'He hasn't asked me.'

'And if he had?'

'I don't know,' she said honestly. 'It would have depended on circumstances, I suppose. I think if you love somebody enough the question of waiting until the wedding night becomes academic. Is that really relevant to what we're talking about?'

'In some respects. It isn't unknown for a man to marry a girl because he can't have her any other way.'

'Now you're being cynical again.'

Surprisingly he smiled a little. 'You could be right. Maybe I overdo it.' He paused, expression uncertain as he studied her. 'If I'm wrong, I'm sorry. It's going to make this thing with Susan that much worse for both of you.'

Jaime flinched but managed to say it levelly. 'You're so convinced Tris is still in love with her?'

'I'm afraid so. I don't think he ever stopped loving her. He just convinced himself he had.'

She spread her hands in a helpless little gesture. 'What should I do?'

He hesitated. 'If you'd asked me that question some minutes ago I'd probably have advised a dignified retreat, with my help. Now ...' he lifted his shoulders ... 'I'm not sure what to advise.'

'Shouldn't Tris be allowed to make up his own mind in his own time?'

'It isn't as simple as that. He's more than capable of deciding he must go through with things the way they are, regardless. He hates letting anybody down.'

'I know,' she said, and swallowed. 'But I'd rather he faced the truth than ruin all our lives.'

'Even if it means losing him altogether?'

'Isn't that what love is about?'

'Ideally, I suppose it is.' Mouth twisting, he indicated her barely touched glass. 'Finish your brandy.'

'That's hardly going to help.'

'No, but it smoothes the rougher edges.' He looked down at his own empty glass and grimaced. 'Like hell it does.' There was a short wait before he spoke again, and when he did his tone had changed. 'Look, Jaime, if I know Susan she's going to come out fighting once she's got over the initial shock. If you do the same thing, Tris is going to be torn in two.'

Her voice felt strangled. 'You'd like me to be the one to step down, is that it?'

'Unless Tris can totally convince you he's over her.'

'That's placing a lot of trust in my judgment.'

He shook his head. 'I don't blame you for feeling bitter. I waded in with a rather heavy hand last night.'

She said wearily, 'You were protecting your family interests, that's all. If I'd been in your shoes two years ago, I'd have probably felt the same way.'

'You've no idea how I felt about it.' The tone was short. 'I remember watching you with that sugar daddy of yours that night and itching to step in and take a swing at him. You'd have benefited from a good slapping yourself, if it comes to that. Something to bring you to your senses before it was too late.'

'You as good as did that by the way you looked at me,' Jaime said low-toned. 'For the first time I saw it from the outside.'

'Yet you still carried on with it.'

'No!' She stopped and bit her lip, sensing his scepticism. 'Oh, what does it matter!'

'Not at all at the moment. Tris has enough on his plate without any further complications.'

Jaime searched the strong features, looking for some sign of tolerance. 'And if you did happen to be wrong about Susan?'

'That's another matter.'

'Meaning you'd continue to hold it over my head.'

'I don't know. I'd have to think about it.' He moved impatiently. 'Just let it ride for a day or two. It isn't going to be easy, whatever happens.'

'But obviously you'd prefer Susan for a sister-in-law.'

Something flickered in the grey eyes. 'I suppose you could say that, yes. Our families have been close for a long time. If you've finished with your drink we'd maybe better think about turning in.' He paused a moment, then added levelly, 'If you'd like to make an early start, I'll show you round the stud before breakfast in the morning. I don't know what Tris will have planned for the rest of the day.'

It was on the tip of her tongue to refuse, but something stopped her. He was making a peace-offering of sorts—perhaps only because he thought he could afford it, but nevertheless it was there.

'What time?' she asked.

'Say seven-thirty.'

Jaime nodded, not trusting herself to speak. She got to her feet unsteadily, placed the half empty glass on a table and walked past him to the door. She could feel his eyes on her, but she couldn't have said goodnight to save her life. There was nothing good about it.

There were times during the following two or three days when Jaime was convinced she had nothing to worry about, others when Tris seemed to sink within himself all over again. Liam kept his own counsel but watched the two of them with cynical appraisal, waiting, Jaime supposed, for something to break. In her heart she knew she should have the courage to force the issue out into the open where it belonged and make Tris face his doubts, but whenever the opportunity presented itself she shied away from it.

She spent some considerable time learning about the stud from Liam's manager, glad to have her mind occupied. Brian Jacobs was a man in his late thirties, quiet and reserved until drawn out of his shell to talk about his beloved charges. For all his knowledge of the animals, he deferred to Liam as the expert, and not wholly, Jaime felt, because he just happened to work for the man.

'He only founded the stud ten years ago,' he said one time. 'In four he'd made the Oakleigh name really come to mean something in the show world. Two of the country's top show jumpers are Oakleigh bred, both sired by Oberon over there.' He gave her an oblique look. 'You'll be learning to ride yourself in time, I suppose?'

Jaime murmured some kind of response and made her escape, wondering bleakly how much the man knew of the present situation. There had been no communication that she knew of from Susan since Sunday evening and Tris had not once mentioned her name, yet she was there constantly between them. She couldn't take much more of this uncertainty, she decided. One way or another, Tris had to sort himself out.

It was Thursday before Liam took a hand in matters again. He chose a time when Tris was otherwise engaged to collar Jaime, putting her in the car on the pretext of running her round to the stud to see the latest new foal, but making instead for the Bakewell road.

'You and I need to talk,' he said firmly, 'and we're better doing it away from the house.' He glanced her way when she remained silent, expression hardening a fraction. 'It's no use closing your mind to it the way you've been doing these last few days. If Tris won't face up to facts, you'll have to do it for the two of you.'

'What do you want me to do?' she asked tonelessly.

'I want you to give him back his ring and tell him you've made a mistake.'

'Just like that. What makes you think he'd believe me?'

'It doesn't matter whether or not he believes you. What he needs is the freedom.'

Her throat hurt. 'He could ask me for that.'

'You know he won't. He considers himself committed to marrying you.'

It was a moment before Jaime could bring herself to say it. 'Did he tell you so?'

'No, he told Susan so.' The pause held deliberation. 'On the phone last night. I overheard the latter part of the conversation by accident. It left me in little doubt as to his true feelings.' The glance came her way again, rapier-swift and thrusting. 'You wouldn't want to marry a man who no longer wants to marry you, would you?'

'No,' she said thickly. 'Always providing you've got it right.'

His sigh was impatient. 'Stop grasping at straws! I don't know whether Susan contacted him first or the other way round, but last night wasn't the first time they'd spoken since Sunday.'

'You seem to have gleaned a lot from a few words. How long were you really listening?'

Liam tightened his mouth and changed down suddenly, spinning the wheel to head into a narrow lane little more than a car's width. When they finally came to a stop they were out of sight of the road and barred by a closed gate from proceeding any further. There were cows in the field beyond, with a view of sloping wooded hillside beyond that again. Liam reached for cigarettes, lighting one for himself when she refused and dropping the glowing coil back into its slot before switching off the ignition.

'I don't want to get too brutal about this,' he said flatly, 'but no way are you going back to town on Sunday with this thing still unresolved. I told you she'd fight. She didn't sink her pride and come all this way back just to see it all go down the drain again.'

Jaime said with bitterness, 'She certainly seems to have enlisted your aid!'

'She didn't ask for it, if that's what you're implying.'

He upended the smouldering cigarette and watched the smoke curl away from the tip with unrelenting eyes. 'Give him up, Jaime. Don't force me into using other methods. This way you come out of it in the best of lights.'

She turned her head to study him for a long moment, seeing the lean, hard profile through a kind of blur. He was wearing a loose suede jacket over a silky yellow sweater, his shoulder almost touching hers as he sat. The hand holding the cigarette was long-fingered and tanned on the back beneath its light coating of dark hair. She knew a sudden swift desire to have him reach out that hand and pull her to him, to feel his lips on hers blotting out thought as they had done the other night, hurting her until the other pain became a dull memory.

'All right,' she said in a voice barely audible. 'You win. But I'll have to do it my way.'

There was no triumph in his face. 'Which way is that?'

'A letter left with the ring. I ... couldn't face him.' She paused numbly. 'There must be an evening train from Chesterfield I could catch.'

'The early one tomorrow would be better.' He revealed no particular reaction. 'I could run you in for it.'

'That means a whole evening to get through. I don't think I could bear that.'

'Then tell him to his face when we get back, then you can leave quite openly for the station.'

'No.'

His shrug held resignation. 'You can't have it both ways. The morning train, then. You'll be in London by ten-thirty.'

Right then Jaime couldn't have cared less where she would be at ten-thirty. She said, 'You realise I won't be going back to Lockharts on Monday, of course. Tris will have to take care of that himself. Be embarrassing for him having to explain things, but I'm sure he'll cope. Better still, you could go and do it for him.'

Liam ignored the last. 'What will you do?'

'Get another job. Good secretaries are in short supply, in case you hadn't heard, and whatever else I might be, I am good at my job.' Her head was up, her chin jutting. 'I shan't have any difficulty.'

'You'll need references. I'll make sure you get them.'

'Don't bother.'

The reply came crisp and short. 'I said you'll get them. What you do with them is your affair.' There was a moment in which he seemed about to add something else, then he apparently changed his mind, stubbing the cigarette in the dashboard tray and reaching forward to switch on the ignition. 'I'm going to have to turn round to get out of here. Nip out and open me that gate, will you.'

Jaime did so without argument, too desolate to care even when her shoes sank deep into the mud as she swung the gate back into the field. The browsing herd was beginning to show a concerted interest by the time Liam had the car reversed and pointing in the right direction. The closer members were already ambling across when she closed the gate and slid back the wire holding it.

Liam watched her get back into the car with a twisted little smile on his lips. 'I think I owe you a new pair of shoes,' he said. 'I hadn't realised you were wearing such flimsy ones.'

'You hardly gave me time to think about changing them,' Jaime heard herself answer, and thought how hollow her voice sounded. 'Put it down to experience—I certainly shall. Anything else I'm likely to toss in the dustbin.'

He kept the engine ticking over but still made no

attempt to move off. His regard held something unfathomable. 'I'll remember that.'

Jaime was to remember that evening as among the worst in her life. It was certainly the longest. At dinner, Tris was talkative and seemingly lighthearted, but one only had to look in his eyes to realise that the laughter was self-delusive.

'Might be an idea if we travelled back Saturday instead of waiting till Sunday,' he suggested at one point. 'Less of a rush.'

Jaime tried to imagine his reaction if she told him now that she would not be here on Saturday, and knew she couldn't bring herself to face it. She felt Liam looking at her but refused to meet his gaze. Right or wrong, she had to do this her own way.

Saying goodnight was an ordeal knowing she would be gone when he woke. Her arrangements with Liam already made, there was nothing else to do but wait for the morning to come. Reaching the temporary haven of her room, she drew a shuddering breath. A bare week ago she had been in a seventh heaven of delight feeling herself loved and wanted by a man she loved in return. Now she had nothing. Had it not been for Susan she could have risked telling Tris about Gerald with a fair chance of having him understand, but it no longer even mattered. All she had been was a substitute for a girl he had believed he would never see again, although she might never have known if things had worked out differently.

Well, they hadn't, she told herself firmly. And the sooner she came to terms with that fact the better. Consign the 'if only' theme to the dustbin and get on with living. She had done it before.

Sleep was out of the question. She packed her suitcase ready for morning, and spent the balance of the night sitting in the armchair overlooking the darkened gardens. At five-thirty, she showered and dressed in the same suit she had worn to travel up in the previous week, applying make-up and brushing her hair more from habit than through any real interest in her appearance.

Liam was leaning against the bonnet of the gleaming blue Mercedes smoking a cigarette when she let herself quietly out of the house. He stubbed it and came forward to take her case from her, opening the nearside door for her to slide into the front seat.

He said nothing when he got in beside her after depositing the suitcase in the boot. Above the Arran-knit white sweater his features looked austere, mouth set in a line which discouraged communication of any kind. Not that Jaime wanted to talk. She just wanted to be on the train and away.

Inevitably she was reminded of the last time she had driven like this with a man through the early morning mists to catch a train for home. Gerald, too, had sat in silence, eyes fixed on the road ahead, but there had been a different quality to it. Liam's manner held no censure. He simply had nothing to add to what had already been said.

They had five minutes to spare on reaching the station. Despite her protests, he insisted on purchasing her a first class ticket and accompanying her on to the platform. When the train came in he put her into a carriage and stashed her suitcase, then looked at her with eyes from which all expression was carefully wiped.

'Good luck,' he said.

'Thanks.' Her voice sounded thick. She clutched her handbag a little tighter as she added, 'I left the letter in my room along with the ring. Are you going to let Tris find it, or shall you tell him first?'

'I'll tell him.' He paused. 'I expect he'll be contacting you.'

'Even if only to express his gratitude for my understanding?' The irony helped. 'I'd rather he didn't.'

Liam made no answer to that. 'Goodbye, Jaime,' he said. 'It's a pity we couldn't have met under different circumstances.'

But that's life, she thought bitterly as he left her. She made no effort to turn her head and look for him on the platform as the train began pulling away.

CHAPTER FOUR

LONDON had never seemed quite so lonely a place as during the following week. With no job to go to, Jaime spent her time either pottering about the flat or walking on the common. Town was out in case she saw someone from the office. She could imagine Gwen Walsh's reaction to the broken engagement—although the cause of it might not please her quite so much if she ever found out.

No one from Lockharts had as yet contacted her in any way, causing her to wonder just what story Tris had put across as a reason for her failure to return. She barely knew whether to be relieved or scornful when he himself failed to get in touch. The way she had left called for some kind of comment from him, surely. It was only common decency.

Hope died hard, she acknowledged at last. At the back of her mind she had been waiting for him to ring and tell her it was all a mistake—that he loved her and only her. Forlorn indeed. She wasn't the kind of girl men loved with any depth, apparently. This would be the last time she risked giving her heart to anyone. It simply wasn't worth the pain.

She was apathetic about looking for a new job, not at all sure what she wanted to do, or even that she wanted to stay in London. A complete change might be good for her, she reasoned, when she could bring herself to think about it at all: a new slant on life. She might be safer working for a female employer—or failing that, a man as happily married as it was possible to be, should such a state exist.

It was this latter, fast-growing cynicism that made her finally decide she rather desperately needed a holiday before anything. She had enough put by for a week or so somewhere. Spending her savings with no immediate prospects of a job smacked of irresponsibility perhaps, but she refused to allow that knowledge to deter her. Her rent here at the flat was paid until the end of the month. After that—well, who could tell? She would worry about later when it came.

She had thought hope totally dead after six days of silence from Tris. It was only on feeling it flare again late on the Thursday afternoon when the knock came on the door that she realised it wasn't and never had been. The sight of the tall, dark-haired man standing outside was like a dash of cold water in the face.

Liam watched the light fade from her eyes with a cynicism of his own. He was dressed for a business trip in a dark grey suit, and carried a briefcase under his arm.

'I've brought you a letter,' he said. 'Tris wanted to come and see you himself, but I managed to persuade him that was the last thing you'd want.' He waited a moment, brows lifting questioningly when she failed to respond. 'May I come in?'

Still without speaking, Jaime stood back to allow him access. He sent a comprehensive glance around the small but nicely furnished room, nodded as if in confirmation of some private observation and turned back to extract an envelope from his briefcase and hand it to her.

'He could have posted it,' she said dully.

'He intended to—or he intended I should do it for him.'

'Then why didn't you?'

'Because I wanted to see you.' He met her swift upward glance levelly. 'It can wait. Read your letter first. I've no idea what it says—he didn't discuss it with me.'

'Would you like some coffee?' she asked. 'I was just going to make some.'

'Very much.' If he realised she needed the privacy of the tiny kitchenette before she opened the letter, he kept it hidden. Liam tossed the briefcase down on to the nearest chair and took a seat on the settee, moving his feet to avoid the low table which took up almost all the room in front of it.

Jaime left him and went through to fill the kettle. Only when it was switched on and two cups set out on the waiting tray did she finally pick up the letter again, turning it over for a brief, lip-biting moment before steeling herself to slit the envelope. The familiar writing tightened the band across her chest almost unbearably. There was just one page:

> *Jaime, What do I say? You must think me the world's biggest heel for letting you go the way I did. When Liam told me, my first impulse was to come after you and fetch you back, then I read your letter and realised you had seen far more deeply and immediately than ever I deserved.*
>
> *Yes, I love Susan. I suppose I've always loved her. I love you too, Jaime, believe me, but I know now that it isn't in quite the same way. When Sue went storming off to visit her aunt and uncle in South Africa it was just a gesture at first. What she really wanted was for me to prove myself by going out after her and fetching her back. I didn't because I was damned if I was going to be the one to crawl, so she stayed on.*
>
> *She's grateful to you, Jaime, as I am too for your*

understanding. Someday I hope you can bring yourself to forgive me.

Don't worry about Lockharts—I've seen to all that. I feel I owe you a great deal, so I'm putting matters in motion to find you another position as good, and hope you will accept. Pride cost Sue and me almost two years. Please don't let it cost you anything—life is too short. Tris.

Liam was sitting where she had left him when she went through with the coffee. He looked up from the magazine he had been flicking through to give her a brief appraisal, but made no comment.

'What did you want to see me about?' she asked abruptly when he had his cup. At this moment all she desperately wanted was to be alone.

'I need your help,' he said, and she jerked her head upright to stare at him.

'I don't...'

'I realise you can't be feeling too well inclined towards any of the Caine family right now,' he interrupted with a faint twist of his lips, 'but I'm hoping to overcome that.' The hesitation seemed uncharacteristic of him. When he did carry on his tone was emotionless. 'A few years ago I was engaged to be married myself. I made the mistake of introducing my fiancée to an American horse breeder I had visiting Oakleigh. When he went back to Kentucky he took her with him.' He shook his head as Jaime opened her mouth to speak. 'No, let me finish. Hal Lessing owns one of the finest studs in the States. Normally he won't sell stock out of the country, but two days ago I had an offer from him of first choice out of a pair of three-year-old fillies. I don't know what made him change his mind after four years, but I want that animal badly enough to put personal feelings to one side. Unfortunately, it means my going out there myself to do the choosing and arrange the shipping.'

'And meet your former fiancée,' Jaime said in quick comprehension. 'I can see that will be awkward, but ...' she paused, brows drawn together in a puzzled frown ... 'I don't see where I come in.'

'I want you to come with me,' he said.

It was a moment before Jaime could find her voice. Her mind felt blank. 'I might be dense,' she got out at last, 'but why on earth would you want to take *me* to America?'

'Pride,' Liam said. There was irony in the line of his mouth. 'Another Caine failing. I need a bolster, if you see what I mean.'

Jaime saw quite clearly. She could even appreciate the motive. Not that it made any difference to her reactions.

'You want someone to act as your girl-friend or something, is that it?' The anger and hurt at his callousness caught her by the throat, thickening her voice. 'I don't know what gave you the idea I might be willing to play that sort of game, but you can think again! Everything else aside, I wouldn't dream of going anywhere with a man I barely know!'

'You'd be perfectly safe,' he said. 'I wouldn't be taking advantage.'

'You won't be getting the chance!' She was on the extreme edge of her chair, eyes blazing. 'Get one of your women friends to do it. I'm sure there must be several who'd jump at the chance!'

'Not without an offer of permanency to go with it.'

'Oh, I see. And that's the last thing you'd want. I suppose you swore off marriage for ever after Lillian let you down!'

His eyes narrowed. 'Who told you her name? I haven't mentioned it.'

That pulled her up for a moment. The use of it had been unintentional, though why she should feel guilty about it she barely knew.

'Tris mentioned it in passing,' she admitted. 'It explained a lot about your attitude—or I thought it did at the time.'

There was sudden mockery in his glance. 'I'm not a misogynist, if that's what you thought. I treat as I find.'

'As you *believe* you find,' she came back scathingly. 'You're about as good a judge of character as one might expect from a bigot!'

'All right, so I'm a bigot.' He sounded unperturbed. 'Right now I'm not particularly concerned with personalities. I'm asking you to do this thing for me because you were the only one I could think of who wouldn't want to make anything of it. You could regard it as a temporary job, plus a holiday rolled into one. Naturally, I'd see to it that you weren't the loser. I know of a secretarial position coming open shortly that would suit you to perfection. My word would be enough to secure it for you.'

'Thanks,' she said with bite. 'Tris is finding me another job.'

'Which you won't accept.' He lifted broad shoulders at the look on her face. 'You wouldn't take anything from Tris now, and you know it. Not that he deserves any better than to have the offer thrown in his face. He's been lucky. You could have made things very uncomfortable for everybody if you'd chosen.'

The anger died. Jaime said dully, 'There wasn't much point in hanging around any longer. It wasn't going to change anything.'

'But some might have done it just the same,' Liam paused, eyeing her consideringly. 'Look, Jaime, I realise I'm asking a lot of you. If you say no I'll have to go anyway. I can't miss this chance. It would just make it easier all round if I went accompanied, that's all.'

Somehow Jaime found herself unable to summon further indignation. She could see his point only too well. She said helplessly, 'It just wouldn't work. I'm not an actress.'

'All women are actresses, one way or another.' His tone was dry. 'It wouldn't call for much. The British aren't renowned for demonstrative behaviour in public, even with their nearest and dearest. Providing you appeared to take pleasure in being with me at all we wouldn't have to get too close.'

She looked at him for a long moment, searching for the words to convince him that it really was impossible to do what he was asking, realising what it must have cost a man like Liam Caine to reveal so much of his inner self. If pride was a sin then so was lack of charity. It wasn't Liam's fault that Tris had let her down. Nor could she really blame him for thinking as he did about that time two years ago. He was a hard man, but she had a feeling he was also a man one might trust to keep his word.

'I don't know,' she heard herself saying without any conscious intention. 'I just don't know.'

'Think about it.' He kept his tone level, betraying no pressure. 'I'm staying in town tonight. Have dinner with me and think about it.'

'Tonight.' She sought for some excuse to say no, and suddenly found she didn't want to say no. For six nights now she had been stuck in this flat on her own thinking about what might have been with her and Tris. She couldn't face another.

'It won't commit you to anything,' Liam assured her, watching her face. 'If you decide against it by the end of the evening I'll accept it. That's a promise.'

'All right.' Jaime had a faint suspicion that she was burning her boats in going even this far, yet found it impossible to back out. 'All right, I'll think about it.'

He became brisk then, glancing at his watch. 'It's half past six now. I'll phone through for reservations somewhere while you change, then we'll get a taxi into town and have a drink before we eat. Okay?'

He had already made the phone call by the time she came out from the kitchen after taking through the tray.

'I've reserved a table for seven-thirty,' he said. 'If we leave here at seven we should be in good time. Is there anywhere round here I might get some cigarettes?'

'There's a newsagents two corners down that might still be open,' Jaime told him.

'Right, I'll pop down now. Won't be long.'

She was almost ready by the time he did get back, the doubts pushed firmly to the back of her mind. Uncertain of where they might be going, she had chosen a silky black trouser suit with long sleeves caught in at the wrist and a high round neckline. Liam helped her on with her jacket without comment on her appearance, but then this was hardly that kind of relationship, she told herself wryly. They were two people poles apart in everything that really counted. Somehow that almost seemed to make his proposition more feasible.

They went to a restaurant somewhere off Piccadilly which Jaime had never heard of before. The place was small and intimately lit, and offered a limited but excellent menu in which the attention to detail turned every dish into a repast fit for a king.

'How did you find it?' Jaime asked after finishing the

best veal papagallo she had ever tasted. 'I must remember the name!' She laughed. 'And the location, of course. Did you ever spend hours in London searching for a restaurant you were sure you could find again without bothering to take down details? I'm sure some of these little places are like Brigadoon and only come back every two hundred years!'

Liam was smiling back, the austerity of his features relieved by the lighting. 'This one is here when I want it, and that's all I worry about. I discovered it about ten years ago quite by accident. Egon Ronay came on it a couple of years back.' He saw her smile fade, and made a small impatient gesture. 'Don't be so sensitive. A whole lot of things happened a couple of years ago, apart from your little affair.'

'It wasn't an affair,' she said sharply. 'Not in the way you mean. Not that I expect you to believe it!'

He studied her for a moment before replying, eyes enigmatic. 'Is it important whether I believe it or not?'

It was, more than she was prepared to admit. She shrugged, and made herself relax again. 'I don't suppose so. It was a long time ago.'

'And we're concerned only with the present,' he agreed. 'Are you still undecided?'

Jaime toyed with her wine glass, watching the pale rose-coloured liquid swirl gently against the sides. 'It isn't an easy decision to make.'

'It wasn't an easy question to ask.'

'No, I realise that.' She looked across at him, seeing him for perhaps the first time with unbiased eyes. Above the paler blur of his shirt, his skin looked tanned and healthy—the face of a man used to spending a great deal of his time out of doors. Attractive, she acknowledged with an odd sense of surprise at the discovery—if one had a leaning towards that kind of hard masculinity. He and Tris were totally different types. No, she mustn't think about Tris. That was over.

'Well?' The dark brows were raised interrogatively, drawing a response before she was fully aware of having made the decision.

'I'll come with you,' she said.

If she had anticipated gratitude she was to be disappointed. He simply nodded. 'Good. I'll make all the arrangements. Can you be ready by Monday?'

'If I have to be.' Jaime was already regretting the decision, knowing he would not be prepared to let her back out so easily now she had said it. He could hardly force her to fly to the States with him, of course, but she hated to think what his reaction might be if she tried to change her mind. Anyway, she reassured herself, look on the bright side. She had wanted a holiday, so count this as a free one. A trip to America was not to be sneezed at, even if certain aspects of it did still worry her a little.

'How long are we likely to be there?' she added.

'Hard to say. A week maybe. I'd like to take the opportunity to have a good look at the stud.'

'I suppose you want this filly for breeding?' Jaime said curiously. 'Why? I thought the Oakleigh strain was second to none.'

'As hunters and potential show animals they're on the top line,' he said. 'Lessing breeds for racing, and he comes up with winners. A foal out of a Rayburn mare by an Oakleigh stallion could come up with all the qualities needed for a world-beater in the jumping ring.'

The light of enthusiasm in his eyes as he spoke changed his whole face, making him look suddenly younger than his thirty-four years. Jaime was aware of a new kind of tension rising within her, faint but unmistakable, and clamped down hard on it. She could not afford to become attracted to another Caine. Not in any way. Once was more than enough!

She made no attempt to invite him in when he took her back to the flat. He told the taxi driver to wait and came with her as far as the main door of the house, opening it for her to pass through into the hallway.

'I'll phone you Sunday morning with the details,' he said. 'Don't let me down, Jaime.'

Was there a hint of a threat in there? she wondered. She returned his gaze with what equability she could muster. 'I won't. Whatever else I might be, I keep my word.'

'Even when you regret having given it?' His lips twitched into a smile. 'It might not be the ordeal you seem to be expecting. Rayburn is a show place, one of the most beautiful houses in the whole of Kentucky, I'm told. You'll like Lessing too. Most women do.'

'For his looks or his money?' It was out before she could stop it. Fatalistically she watched the hardness come down like a shutter over his face.

'Depends which priority matters most. He has both. Try sorting yours out over the weekend, will you?'

She asked for that, she thought ruefully on her way upstairs to the first floor. If she was going to go through with this thing she had to do it wholeheartedly. *If* she was going through with it? That was a laugh. Try getting out of it now!

The flight was long and tiring but uneventful. So uneventful in fact that Jaime was bored practically to tears before it was halfway over. At intervals she fingered the unfamiliar bulk of the antique sapphire and diamond ring

Liam had slid on to her finger at the airport that morning. My mother's, he had said briefly. Might be a bit large, but that can't be helped. We didn't get round to having it altered yet.

She slid a glance his way now, sitting on her left in the comfortable first class section of the 747, head back against the rest. Impossible to tell what thoughts were going on behind those grey eyes. She wasn't at all sure she even wanted to know.

As if sensing her regard, Liam turned his head to look back at her brows lifting in the fast-becoming-familiar mockery.

'Finished your book?'

'As much of it as I feel like reading.' She reached up and adjusted the air flow for about the hundredth time. 'It feels so stuffy in here!'

'Pressurised cabins always do. Most people get used to it after a time. Sorry your first flight had to be a long one.'

Jaime stopped fiddling abruptly. 'Is it so obvious?'

'Frankly, yes. Nothing to be ashamed of. We can't all be seasoned travellers. Would you like to go up to the cocktail lounge?'

She shook her head, looking out through the window at the cloud fields piled up under the plane. 'It wouldn't be so bad if there were something to see!'

'Apart from the Atlantic and an occasional ship, you still wouldn't see anything if this lot cleared,' he came back reasonably. 'Try listening to the radio. Music soothes.'

'It's canned.'

'What did you expect, Radio Three?'

Jaime stiffened, then as suddenly relaxed, mouth twitching into a smile despite herself. 'You're right, I'm nit-picking. Nerves probably. I keep remembering we're at thirty-six thousand feet.'

'Not for much longer. Another hour or so and we'll be starting the descent towards the coast.'

New York. Jaime drew in a long slow breath. There were compensations attached to this arrangement of theirs. She had always wanted to travel, yet never done a great deal about it. If she could find a new job involving travel when she returned home it might be well worth considering. Not that she supposed they were all that easy to come by.

Lockharts had sent through her cards and a cheque for salary owed her to date. The letter accompanying had been stiff and formal, making no comment whatsoever on her lack of notice. She hoped they would have no difficulty in filling her position. Letting people down was not in her line either.

'Will Tris be staying in London now?' she forced herself to ask.

Liam shook his head. 'He's going to come home and start running the financial side of the estate.'

'Leaving you more time to spend with your horses.'

'Can't say I've ever really lacked it. The estate manager does a good job. Pity you never met Tom Reading. He was away last week visiting his folks.'

Jaime waited for the shaft of pain to strike through her at the mention of those days she had spent at Oakleigh, but could summon little emotion. Something had gone from her since receiving the letter, leaving her empty of any kind of feeling over Tris at all. Perhaps she hadn't been as much in love with him as she had imagined: self-delusion could work both ways. Anyway, it was over now and done with. Best to put it out of her mind altogether. Except that sitting here now right next to his brother hardly made that feasible.

But this was only temporary, she reminded herself. Once back in England she need never have cause to think of the Caines again. Meanwhile she would make the most of a trip she might never have the opportunity to repeat.

They landed at Kennedy around eight New York time, and took a cab down-town to their hotel for the night. Seeing the famous Manhattan skyline for the first time proved something of an anti-climax. Better approached by ship, Liam said.

Their rooms were adjoining, with a connecting door bolted from both sides. Jaime looked from her window on the sparkling, scintillating panorama spread out before her and wished she were here on some other pretext. Whatever the reasons, they were both of them preparing to live out a lie.

It still seemed odd to her that a man like Liam Caine should have need of this kind of bolster to his self-esteem. Had she been asked she would have said he was more the type to weather any situation alone. It just went to show that no one was entirely as they appeared on the surface.

She had expected to stay in the hotel for dinner that evening, but Liam had other ideas. They took a cab and cruised the neon-lit thoroughfares for Jaime's benefit first, to the studied indifference of the driver who had heard all the exclamations before. Seated eventually at a table for two in the night-club Liam had chosen, she listened to him ordering food and wine and envied him his ability to dissemble. In no way could she forget why they were here together.

'You seem to know New York pretty well,' she said over coffee, and he smiled and lifted his shoulders.

'Only from memory. I was celebrating my twenty-third birthday last time I was here.'

'Has it changed much?'

'In some respects, not in others.' He paused, eyeing

her, darkly attractive in the olive green lounge suit. 'We could have gone through tonight and stayed in Marysville. I thought you might enjoy a night out on the town, that's all.'

'I am,' she assured him. 'And thank you for thinking of it.'

'The least I could do considering what you're doing for me. There's no adequate recompense for a week out of your life!'

She said with some hesitation, 'You know, I barely know anything about you. Supposing I'm asked a question I can't answer?'

'There's no reason why anybody should question you,' he returned easily. 'Even if they do it's more likely to be general than personal. You've seen Oakleigh, and heard enough about the general set-up.'

'I know nothing at all about horses, though, which might seem rather strange.'

'Life doesn't always tie everything up as neatly as that. Perhaps I fell in love with you despite myself.' There was irony in his smile. 'We met only a few weeks ago and we'll be married this coming summer. Do you see yourself married to me?'

She thought of the night he had kissed her, remembering the hardness of his hands and mouth, the punishing quality of his anger. A quiver ran through her. 'No, I don't,' she said. 'I think you'd want to dominate a woman far too much.'

'That would depend on the woman.' He indicated the dance floor with a nod of his head. 'Shall we?'

Jaime wanted to say no, but something else in her had her on her feet and accompanying him before she could think of a reasonable excuse. He held her lightly at first until the music changed tempo, then drew her in with deliberation, both hands at her back. His breath stirred her hair at the temple, reminding her of similar occasions when she had danced with his brother, except that Tristan's mouth had been more on a level with her cheek.

Awareness grew in her, despite all she could do to try to ignore it, sensitising her to the subtle masculine scent of him, the texture of his skin; the warmth and hardness of his body against her. She tried to pull a little further away from him but was held by the firm pressure of his hands down her spine.

'What are you afraid of?' he asked softly. 'You've been this close to a man before.'

This close but never this unsure of herself, she thought with a growing desperation. It was purely physical, of course—a chemistry one could not control. She wanted to get away from him, but where did she go? Without Liam she was stranded.

'I'd like to sit down,' she said, and was hard put to keep a note of pleading from her voice. 'You realise it's really about four in the morning by our standards?'

'Time we were leaving,' he agreed. 'You don't need to be up too early in the morning. Our flight isn't until noon. I'll order breakfast brought up for both of us.'

Jaime was quiet in the cab taking them back to the hotel. Liam made no attempt to touch her, but she could feel his presence right there at her side. The lobby was busy, with several late arrivals taking up space at the desk. Liam secured both their keys and led the way to the lifts without bothering to hand hers over, giving their floor number to the car attendant and standing behind Jaime as they travelled swiftly upwards.

Reaching her door, he opened it for her, then withdrew the key and put it in her hand with a faint smile. 'No strings attached?'

She remained where she was, gazing up at him with darkened eyes, not sure what it was she wanted until she saw his own expression change and felt his hands come down on her shoulders, drawing her towards him. The touch of his lips brought a weakness to her limbs. Response surged through her, blotting out everything but the moment, moving her closer to him in search of the emotion denied her by his brother.

Still holding her, Liam disengaged himself long enough to push open the door and draw her through into the dimly illuminated room. She felt him take the velvet jacket from her shoulders and the leap of her pulses as he turned her back into his arms.

This time his mouth was rougher, more demanding, his hand moving up to cup and caress the firm curve of her breast through the clinging material of her dress. She made no move to stop him when he slid down the narrow strap over her shoulder, wanting his caresses as she had never wanted anything before, wanting *him* with an abandonment she was later to remember with burning shame.

It was Liam himself who brought her to her senses, holding her away from him in a grip that hurt, eyes glittering with contempt as he moved them over her.

'You damned little tramp!' he said. 'How far down the list would *I* come?'

Jaime was white-faced, shaken to the marrow by the realisation of what she had done—or been ready to do. She tried to straighten herself, but the way he was holding her stopped her, forcing her to abandon the attempt.

'Liam ... please ...' she whispered, and saw his upper lip curl.

'No, stay that way. It suits you. Me too. I merit *some* pleasure out of this.'

'Don't!' She was close to tears, her whole body trembling. 'Let me go, Liam!'

There was a moment when he didn't move, then abruptly he obliged, watching her adjust her dress with sardonic deliberation. 'What comes next?' he asked. 'Or is it too new an experience for you, to be turned down?'

Jaime hit out at him blindly, only to have her wrist caught and held in a crushing grasp. Breath coming in shuddering little gasps, she jerked it free again, closing her fingers about the bruised bone and hugging it against her waist. 'You swine!' she got out.

'You called me that once before,' he said. 'Third time might be unlucky. As I said the other night, I treat as I find.' He paused, then gave a sudden harsh laugh. 'I've got to admit you almost had me taken in with that virginal act. I was even ready to believe you might be telling the truth over that time in Ashbourne. Some joke! Just how many men have had you?'

It was a whisper, forced out from a throat so constricted she could scarcely breathe. 'You're not being fair!'

'Fair about what? That was no innocent response just now. You knew just what you wanted.'

There was too much truth in that to deny with conviction. She gazed at him helplessly, lower lip caught between her teeth. It was no use trying to explain. How could she explain when she didn't even understand herself?

He shrugged when he saw she wasn't going to reply, and moved back to the door. 'We leave for the airport at eleven. Be ready.'

Jaime's own pride lifted sharply. 'If you think I'm still prepared to carry on with this you've got another think coming! I don't even know why I've come this far!'

'We both know why,' he said. 'You just spelled it out. If you can't have one brother try for the other! What was the plan—to give me just enough to make me want more, then hold out for marriage?' The tone seared. 'You must have a lot of confidence in your know-how. Maybe I should have let you carry on!'

'Get out,' she said tautly. 'Just get out of here!'

'Don't worry, I'll go. But make no mistake about it, you're coming with me on that plane.'

'To save your damned pride? Why should I care about that any more?' Her voice was ragged. 'If you force me to go with you to Rayburn I'll tell them all the truth about why I'm there. I mean it, Liam!'

'You do,' he said softly, 'and you'll rue the day you ever set eyes on the Caine family.'

'Do you think I don't already?'

'Not half as much as you would. I'll leave you to consider it.'

He was gone several minutes before Jaime could bring herself to move. She felt sick. What had happened had been her fault and hers entirely. She had wanted Liam to make love to her. But that didn't make her a tramp—or a liar. Just a fool who couldn't see straight.

CHAPTER FIVE

THERE was a chauffeur-driven car to meet them at the airport in Marysville, long, sleek and luxuriously upholstered. Seated in the rear as they left the town and sped through lush green pastureland, Jaime consoled herself with the thought that she would only be here a short time. Whatever her feelings towards the man at her side might have been before, she detested him now with an intensity that gave her a kind of strength. She only wished she had the courage to carry out her threat, but knew herself incapable of putting *his* word to the test. She had a feeling his retaliatory urges would know few limits.

Rayburn was as beautiful as she had been led to expect, a great white curve of a house supported by classical pillars. Somehow Jaime had taken it for granted that Hal Lessing would be about Liam's own age, but the man who came out to greet them was in his late fifties, though exceedingly fit-looking, his face fleshless, hard-boned and angular under a sweep of iron-grey hair. His eyes gave the lie to first impressions, however. Dark brown and warm with humour, they seemed to belong in another setting.

'Sorry I couldn't get to meet you in person,' he said when greetings were over. 'I was expecting a phone call.' His voice was deep and slow with a pronounced Kentucky drawl Jaime found entrancing. 'Lillian's around somewhere. Guess she didn't hear the car.'

He went on talking as they entered the house through

wide oak doors into a great hallway. A white-balustered staircase swept grandly up to the next floor, reminding Jaime of the one in *Gone With The Wind* which she had seen a few months back. The whole house was of that era. One almost expected to see Rhett Butler standing at the foot gazing sardonically up at the head-tossing Scarlett.

Their luggage disappeared in the direction of the upper regions in the grip of a young, white-coated Negro servant, leaving the two of them to follow their host through to a spacious drawing room decorated in red and gold with a magnificent chandelier as a centrepiece. Floor-length windows gave on to a view of formal gardens stretching to infinity.

Jaime could sense no particular reaction in Liam as the woman standing by the far window turned on their entry, coming towards them with outstretched hand and a smile which looked every inch genuine.

'Liam!' she exclaimed. 'Lovely to see you again! It's been so long!'

Liam took the hands held out to him, his own smile surprisingly easy and unstrained. 'You haven't altered at all, Lillian.' He remained for a fleeting moment looking down into the striking face under its cloud of dark hair before releasing her to turn and draw a reluctant Jaime forward, his arm firmly about her shoulders. 'I'm hoping you two will keep one another company while Hal shows me around.'

It could have been imagination on Jaime's part which caused her to see the vivid blue eyes harden a fraction. Certainly the other's expression remained welcoming enough.

'What a good idea,' she said. 'I could do with a little light relief from eternal horse talk.' She didn't look directly at her husband, but from the way he stiffened the remark seemed intended to hurt. 'I hope you're not a fanatic too?'

'Jaime doesn't know one end of a horse from another,' said Liam, and deliberately tightened his grip to draw her closer. 'I haven't had time yet to start teaching her to ride. Perhaps she could make a start while we're here.'

'I might as well wait until we're back home again,' she came back coolly, determined not to be railroaded into anything. 'There's hardly going to be time for riding lessons.'

Hal smiled at her. 'Hope you'll both feel free to stay as long as you like. Glad to have you.' He turned as yet another of the white-coated servants pushed a loaded trolley into the room. 'Ah, here's tea. Lillian thought you might appreciate it after the flight down.'

'I was never more ready for a cup in my life,' Jaime admitted. 'It's very thoughtful of you.'

'Oh, I refuse to become totally Americanised,' Lillian said with that same silky emphasis. 'Tea at four, dinner at eight. That's civilised!'

Hal took a seat alongside Jaime on a long chesterfield. 'Is this your first trip to the States?' he asked.

She refrained from stating dryly that it was also her last, and nodded. 'I wasn't expecting to come,' she said with truth. 'Liam only suggested it at the last moment.'

'Yet you managed it.' His smile held an underlying irony. 'Most women would need more notice.'

'Oh, I don't know. Packing a suitcase doesn't take long. And when the incentive is there ...' She broke off, not sure what her own incentive had been any more. 'Anyway, I'm here,' she finished lamely.

'And very welcome. Good for Lillian to have someone from her own country around for a time. She misses

England.' Hal spoke in a lowish tone as if he didn't want what he was saying to carry across to his wife who was talking animatedly with Liam as she organised cups and saucers. He added on a curious note, 'How did you come to meet Liam if you've no interest in horses? Mostly we breeders tend to move in our own circles.'

Jaime wondered what his reaction would be if she told him she had been engaged to Liam's brother Tris less than two weeks ago. 'At a party,' she improvised. 'I was staying with mutual friends in Derbyshire and they introduced us.' She sensed Liam was listening and hoped he appreciated her efforts on his behalf. 'Nobody was more surprised than I was when he asked me to marry him. I can't even claim a childhood rapport with seaside donkeys.'

'Oh, yes, I've seen those,' said Hal, taking her seriously. 'Pitiful little beasts. Never could understand how a nation of so-called animal-lovers can rationalise that kind of set-up.'

Jaime smiled and shrugged. 'Oh, we're top of the league at turning a blind eye.'

Liam said levelly, 'There are pretty strict laws governing the use of donkeys for amusement. They're not as badly done to as their expressions suggest. Don't let Jaime fool you, Hal. She's British enough to enjoy self-abasement.'

'Don't generalise, darling,' Lillian put in smoothly. 'We don't all run ourselves down. Cream, Jaime?'

'Please.' There was no way of answering her snide little insinuation, but it stung. Trust Liam to make something out of a simple meaningless joke!

Hal appeared not to have noticed any change in atmosphere. 'We're having a few people over tonight,' he said. 'Hope you can stand it after that journey. Usually takes me a couple of days to adjust to time differences.'

'You travel a lot?' Jaime asked.

'Not so much these days. Get to my age you start realising home's the best place to be.'

She laughed. 'I think you're putting me on—unless you're a great deal older than you look.'

'I'm fifty-nine,' he said. 'Keep that line up and we'll get along just fine!' His glance went smilingly to where Liam sat, his voice lifting as he said, 'You found yourself quite a girl here.'

'Didn't I?' came the dry reply.

Lillian got to her feet when Hal wanted to send for one of the houseboys to show them to their rooms after they'd finished tea.

'I'm going up anyway,' she said. 'I may as well do it myself.'

Jaime was dropped off first, finding her suitcase already unpacked and removed. The room was large, and like everything else in this lovely house, magnificently furnished. 'Exported from England,' Lillian said of the fourposter bed. The smile did not reach her eyes. 'About the same time he brought me over. You're across the landing, Liam.'

There was something not quite right with the Lessings' relationship, Jaime decided thoughtfully when she was alone. The atmosphere between them seemed so brittle—more so on Lillian's part. She was certainly no more than twenty-eight or nine, which made a thirty-year difference at least. Yet four years ago the gap would have been the same.

She tried to imagine herself now at twenty-four marrying a man of fifty-five, and found it difficult. There was so much more than just a gap of years to consider, there was the difference in viewpoints, in inclinations—even surely in the degree of physical need? Did Lillian regret sacrificing one man's prime for an older man's money—or was she herself reading far too much into a few insignificant remarks? The latter seemed likely. How could one assess a whole relationship in bare moments?

The impression persisted, however, during the evening. Hal's few people turned into a dinner party for a dozen. Seated on his right at the long mahogany table, Jaime looked down to where Liam sat in the same position by Lillian's side and wondered what they were talking about with heads so conspiratorially close. The latter looked superb in an emerald green gown, which left her smooth shoulders bare, dark hair swept up and away from her face. Liam seemed mesmerised by the vision and willing enough to be so. He was laughing at the moment, making no attempt to disengage the hand which lay under the scarlet-tipped fingers of his hostess on the white cloth.

'When do you two hope to be married?' Hal asked quietly, and she realised he had been watching her watching them. His expression gave nothing away.

'In the summer,' she said, recalling what Liam had told her. She felt guilty in deceiving this man the way they were, yet what other alternative did she have?

'Think you'll be able to settle at a place like Oakleigh?' he asked next. 'It must be a very different life from the one you're used to leading.'

The answer came without thinking. 'But I'll have Liam.'

The pause lay heavily between them. His sigh when it came was only just audible. 'Yes, you will. Love makes a difference.'

Only if it's shared, she thought, and knew she had put her finger on Hal's problem. Here was a man who had been married for his money and knew it. Perhaps there had been a time when Lillian had taken the trouble to keep up a pretence of loving him back, but not any more. She had made that too obvious this afternoon. Thinly disguised contempt might be closer the mark. Yet Hal scarcely seemed the kind to deserve it.

She hardly saw Liam at all after dinner, though she was certainly not short of company. Not all the Lessings' guests were horse enthusiasts in the same sense, although most of those Jaime spoke with confessed to an interest of one kind or another in the racing world.

'You'll have to pay a visit to the track while you're here,' one man observed. 'Back one winner and you'll know what all the excitement's about. Hal has the best of it, though. He leads a lot of them in. Barely a meeting without he has a winner. It's an obsession with him.'

'Compensation,' murmured his wife half under her breath. Her eyes were on Lillian across the room talking with Liam and another man whose name Jaime could not remember. 'I heard somebody say how Hal's wife knew your fiancé in England before he married her?'

'That's right.' Jaime kept her tone carefully neutral. It was obvious from the way this woman spoke that there was little love lost. Her husband was looking uncomfortable.

'Time we were going,' he said. 'It's getting late.' To Jaime he added pleasantly, 'Hope you enjoy your stay. Are you going to be here long?'

She shook her head. 'Only as long as it takes Liam to arrange shipping for the filly he's buying.'

'To England?' He looked and sounded taken aback. 'First time Hal's let that happen.'

'Perhaps he just never found the right kind of buyer before,' she returned lightly.

That first departure signalled the beginning of the end of the evening. After seeing off the last couple to leave,

Hal came back to the drawing room with an air of relief.

'Nice to see people,' he said with a dry little smile, 'but sometimes even nicer to see them go. Present company excepted, of course. How about a quiet nightcap for the four of us?'

'Not for me, thanks,' Liam said easily. 'An early night wouldn't come amiss, if you can call this so early.'

'It's gone the witching hour.' Lillian's tone was lazy. 'Don't forget our ride in the morning.' Her gaze moved to Jaime and took on a hint of mockery. 'Of course, you don't, do you? That's a pity. I promise to bring him back in time for breakfast.'

Jaime made herself smile. 'Thanks.' She avoided Liam's eye. 'I think I'll go up too. I need to catch up on some sleep.'

Liam put an arm about her shoulders in what she privately thought an unnecessary gesture as they took their leave. He removed it again the moment they were outside the room, and mounted the stairs without touching her in any way. Jaime waited until she reached her bedroom door before turning her head to give him a cold, hard glance.

'Well,' she said, 'how am I doing?'

'To the manner born,' he came back dryly. 'What do you want, a pat on the back?'

She flushed but managed to answer with reasonable calm. 'A quick termination is all I ask for. I hope you're not planning on dragging this thing out.'

His eyes narrowed. 'Any reason why I should?'

'I don't know. Ask yourself.'

He reached out as she made to turn into the room, catching her by the wrist and swinging her back to face him again. His face was hard.

'What are you getting at?'

'Nothing much,' she said recklessly. 'Lillian is a bored woman more than ready for some diversion, but you want that filly. I doubt if you'll put that at risk for the sake of *any* woman.'

The look he gave her was cold and glinting. 'We've been here less than twelve hours. That's a whole lot to surmise in a short time.'

'There's nothing wrong with my eyes,' she came back. 'You were round one another's necks the moment you met—and I wasn't the only one to notice how much time you spent together this evening!'

'About the same as you spent with Hal, I'd say.'

'Isn't that what I'm here for?'

'You know why you're here.'

'To save your pride,' Jaime said scathingly. 'I might have believed that once, but not any more. Personally I don't think you have any. One click of her fingers and she has you turning cartwheels for her!'

There was a short expectant silence, then surprisingly he laughed. 'You're really getting the feel of the part,' he said. 'Jealousy and all! Pity so much talent had to be wasted.' He let her go, mouth curling. 'Don't let all this go to your head. The arrangement is strictly temporary. See you in the morning.'

There was little Jaime could do but accept the dismissal as he moved away across the corridor. They could hardly carry on a slanging match at a distance in someone else's home. She was seething inside, yet oddly disturbed too. In no way was she jealous, she told herself with emphasis. She had no basis for that emotion. She detested Liam Caine with all her heart and soul.

The morning was bright, the sky dotted with high white cloud moving briskly before a wind scarcely evident at ground level.

From her window, Jaime looked out on rolling green paddocks dotted with animals already out to grass. Some had foals with them, long-legged and still ungainly creatures that bore little resemblance to the graceful parents. She supposed there would be more births to come. Spring was the time for it in the animal world. Only the human race staggered its population increases throughout the year.

Hal was already down and eating in the small dining room adjacent to the magnificent main one they had used the night before. He was dressed in cavalry twill slacks and a toning shirt with a paisley scarf tucked into the neckline, grey hair brushed back from the strong features.

'Hope you don't mind my starting,' he said. 'It's a serve-yourself affair here. The others shouldn't be long. They went out at seven.'

It was gone eight-fifteen now. Quite a lengthy morning ride, Jaime reflected, and schooled herself to indifference. Why should it matter to her?

It mattered to Hal, though, she realised when he glanced surreptitiously at his watch a couple of times during the following minutes. For his sake, she was glad to hear voices out in the hall and see the missing pair come through the door.

'Sorry we're late,' said Lillian, not sounding it. 'It's such a glorious morning we went further than we intended.' She looked good in the tailored jodhpurs and fine-knit sweater, and she knew it, her eyes meeting Jaime's across the table as she sat down with an air of satisfaction. 'Sleep well?'

'Fine.' It was all Jaime could find it in her to say. She was aware of Liam's tall, broad-shouldered figure sliding into the chair next to hers, and stiffened as he leaned over to put his lips to her cheek.

'Morning, darling. Not properly awake yet?'

Skin tingling, she resisted the urge to jerk her head away from him, and knew he sensed her reaction when he smiled.

'I've been awake for over an hour,' she said. 'Did you enjoy your ride?'

'Fine.' The smile still lingered. 'Pity you couldn't have joined us. Hal too.'

'I do my riding a bit later on in the day,' returned the older man gruffly. 'The spirit's willing but the flesh doesn't go along. We'll take a look at those two fillies after you finish eating, Liam. No rush to decide, of course. Take your time. There's a race meet on at the Marysville track tomorrow, by the way. Like to go?'

'Are you running anything?'

'A two-year-old—colt called Rebel Lad. First time out. I'm bringing him on for the Champagne Stakes. He'll win it too.'

'I'd like to see him go,' said Liam. 'How about you, Jaime? Any interest in racing?'

'Enough to make me curious.' She looked at Hal. 'Shall I be entitled to bet on him?'

He laughed. 'Every reason why you should! He'll win his race. There's nothing to beat him at this level.'

'You said that about Hybrand last year,' his wife put in, and the grey head jerked.

'I was deluding myself. He had the speed but no staying power. Rebel has both. He'll take the Classic next year.'

'I hope you're right.' There was a lack of both sincerity and real interest in her voice. She drained her coffee cup and pushed back her chair. 'I'm going to change. It's warm enough for the pool if you want to join me later on?' This last with a glance in Jaime's direction. 'You do swim, I suppose?'

Jaime said levelly, 'Yes, I do, but I think I might go along with Liam and learn something about horses this morning.' She looked at Hal with enquiring eyes. 'If I may?'

'You're more than welcome,' he assured her. 'We'll take the car down to the training yard after having a look at the fillies and you can see what I'm talking about. Okay with you, Liam?'

'Fine.' If it wasn't he was giving nothing away.

Lillian left the room without speaking again, mouth compressed. Jaime guessed her annoyed over the way things had worked out and felt a fleeting if unworthy satisfaction. Madame Lessing was too well accustomed to organising people her way. It was time she realised that she, Jaime, was not going to be so dealt with.

The corduroy jeans and plain white shirt she was wearing seemed adequate to the occasion. She walked out between the two men feeling slightly happier than she had earlier. Hal had both fillies in one of the closer paddocks, but they took the car anyway as they would be going on from there.

Jaime had to acknowledge it was a beautiful sight as they slowed to a halt between the two rows of parallel white fences and looked out at the grazing animals. The colours were varied, ranging from a deep chestnut which gleamed richly in the sun through to a dappled grey which shone almost silver when the light caught it.

Hal named the latter for them. 'White Lady. That's Rebel's dam. His sire is a chestnut, Cobbler's Way. Won three Classics for me before I put him to stud. Rebel came out a roan. Just about inevitable from that combination, I reckon.'

Jaime didn't like to ask what colour a roan was, and it apparently occurred to neither man that she might not know. 'I never really appreciated the difference between ordinary everyday horses and thoroughbreds before,' she said. 'They really are superb!'

Hal grinned. 'Better than Oakleigh's?'

'Say yes,' Liam warned on a light note, 'and you'll rue it!'

'I leave the finer points to those in the know,' Jaime said, resisting a desire to kick him on the shin. 'They all look good to me.'

Hal glanced from one to the other of them, an odd expression in his eyes. 'Diplomacy?' he asked.

'Cowardice,' she retorted. 'He beats his women when they disagree with him.'

Liam's smile was dry. 'It's not a bad idea. Which are the two I'm choosing from, Hal?'

'The sorrel over there and the bay in the far corner. I'll have them brought in for a closer look, naturally. Just thought you might like a long view first. The sorrel's Morning Star, the bay Dark Star. Same sire as Rebel, both of them. Ran last season but didn't do much.'

'Is that the reason you're selling them?' Jaime asked, and drew a smile which had a certain reticence about it.

'Can't think of a better. I breed for winners both sides. That way I stand a fair chance of maintaining the Lessing reputation.' He straightened away from the fence, lifting the foot he had been propping to the ground. 'Let's go and take a look at Rebel. These two will be ready for inspection by the time we get back.'

It took them several minutes' driving to reach the training yard. The trainer came over to greet them. He was a man in his late forties, short and stocky with a ragged, stoic look about his features. An ex-jockey? Jaime wondered.

The smell of horseflesh hung on the air as they approached the first line of boxes, pungent but not unpleasant. Rebel Lad was halfway down the row in one of the larger boxes, head stuck inquisitively over the half door at the sound of footsteps. He was already wearing a headcollar. The trainer took hold of it by the strap as he opened the bottom half of the door to lead the animal out on to the wide walkway.

A roan, Jaime saw, was a dark chestnut splashed with spots of grey and white. He was a fine big colt with a beautiful head and powerfully muscled quarters. He blew softly on his handler and nuzzled at his sleeve.

'Why do you call him Rebel?' she asked as Liam walked round the horse with a professional eye. 'He seems to have a lovely nature.'

'He isn't nasty,' said Hal, 'just wayward at times. Needs a strong hand to keep him pointing in the right direction when the mood takes him.' He was watching Liam, a faint smile on his lips at the other man's obvious approval. 'Good?'

'Very nice,' came the agreement with typical British understatement. He patted the gleaming neck, feeling the muscle beneath his fingers. 'I'd like to see him take the Classic.'

'You'll have to come over for it—both of you.' Hal paused, almost with deliberation. 'I guess you'll be married by then—maybe even on the way to a family.'

Jaime caught Liam's sardonic glance and felt the colour tinge her cheeks. This was getting worse. She hated deceiving the man who had been so kind to them both. And why was it necessary anyway? Not for Liam's sake, that was for certain. He couldn't care less what might be thought. So why *was* she here?

'Doubt if we'll be starting a family right away,' he said easily. 'Plenty of time.'

'That's what I said when I married my first wife,' came

the gruff reply. 'Not always as much time as you think.' There was discomfiture in the brown eyes as he looked at the other. 'A man needs a son.'

Was that one of the reasons he had chosen a second wife so much younger than himself? Jaime wondered as the colt was returned to his box. Could he have been hoping for the child a woman his own age could not give him? Yet surely he must have realised that Lillian was hardly the type to want that kind of domesticity?

She excused herself from viewing the two fillies back at the stud, electing instead to walk the comparatively short distance up to the house. She was hot by the time she reached it. On impulse she went up to her room and changed into the swimsuit she had packed at the last minute for no reason other than covering all eventualities, taking a towel with her from the bathroom to go down to the sun-trap of a pool set at the back of the house.

There was no sign of Lillian when she reached it, although loungers were set ready in one corner. Only on putting in a toe to test the temperature of the water did she realise it was heated. That made things perfect. Despite the warmth of the sun these last two days, spring was not yet ready to turn into summer. She dived in with a will and swam a length under water, enjoying the silky caress of it against her skin.

Lillian was sitting waiting for her when she surfaced. She was fully dressed in a woven skirt and top which looked simple enough to be wildly expensive, dark hair framing the vivid face.

'I saw you coming down from the house,' she said as Jaime trod water below her. 'I thought you wanted to be with the men this morning?'

Jaime caught at the side and hauled herself out before

answering, shaking the excess water from her hair and reaching for the towel she had left slung over one of the loungers.

'I thought they might appreciate some time on their own,' she said. 'Especially while Liam decides which animal he wants to buy.'

'He could always take them both.'

'I don't believe he has the option. Your husband said ...'

'My husband says what I want him to say.' The words were soft but underlined. 'Who do you think persuaded him to change the ruling of a lifetime and allow one of his precious horses to go breeding outside the country?'

Jaime stared at her, towel suspended. 'You mean it wasn't his own idea to let Liam buy one of those fillies?' she got out stupidly at length, and saw Lillian's lip curl.

'Isn't that what I just said? Hal likes all things American to stay that way—especially his damned horses! It took me a long time to convince him he owed Liam that much at least.'

Jaime returned her gaze with a steadiness she was long way from feeling. 'Because he took you from him?'

Something flickered in the other eyes. 'Did Liam tell you that, or was it someone else?'

'As a matter of fact, it was his brother.'

'Oh, yes.' The smile was reminiscent. 'How is Tristan?'

'Fine last time I saw him.' Jaime felt nothing. Her brief engagement to Liam's brother was like something that had happened in another lifetime. She was more concerned with this one right now. She added caustically, 'It took you a long time to start feeling you owed Liam something yourself.'

'Nobody likes to admit to making a mistake. I've tried to make a go of it with Hal, but it just hasn't worked out.'

'And you thought if you could get Liam over here you could take up where you left off and let him get you out of it?'

'Something like that.' There was no trace of discomfiture. 'Of course, I wasn't to know he'd acquired himself a fiancée.'

'That rather cuts you down to size, doesn't it?'

'Not at all. He's not in love with you.'

Jaime was dismayed by the strength of her reaction to that statement. She took a grip on herself with an effort. 'Is that what he told you?'

'Not in so many words. But I'm a woman, darling, I can read between the lines. He's proud of the family name and wants to perpetuate it. For that he needs a wife.'

Wrong lines, Jaime thought dryly. Aloud she said, 'There's Tristan. He's going to be married soon.'

'Hardly the same thing, though, is it? As the eldest, Liam will want to hand over control to his own son.'

'Which you'd have been prepared to give him if you'd married him?'

'In time. That wasn't the only reason he wanted to marry *me*.'

'You're only guessing it's the reason he wants to marry me. You don't *know* how he feels.'

Lillian laughed, a short mocking sound which set Jaime's teeth on edge. 'I know how a man looks at a woman when he's in love with her, and it isn't the way he looks at you. Which leaves us with what? That he couldn't have you any other way? Hardly likely. If he wanted you that badly he'd not be doing any waiting. Not the Liam I knew!'

'Four years ago.'

'People don't change to any great extent. Specially not men.'

'I'm sure you're an expert.' The moment she had said it Jaime regretted it. Why stoop to her level? She wrapped the towel around herself, stilling an inclination to shiver in the air which felt cool now after her immersion in warm water. 'I don't know why you're telling me all this, it doesn't do anybody any good. You'd still be married to Hal if I weren't engaged to Liam.'

'There's such a thing as divorce.'

'He might not be prepared to marry a divorcee.'

The laugh came again. 'Honey, so long as we were both free he wouldn't care. He made that fairly clear this morning. Where do you think we were all that time?'

Jaime thought of Hal sitting there looking at his watch while he waited and wanted to slap the beautiful uncaring face in front of her now. What she wanted to do to Liam was something else. He had accepted Hal's hospitality and peace-offering, but saw nothing wrong in making love to his wife less than twenty-four hours after getting here. Love? Why soil the word? He and Lillian were two of a kind. They deserved one another. So far as she was concerned they were welcome, but what about Hal? He deserved better.

'What you're suggesting is I give him up?' she said bluntly, playing for time, though to what purpose she had no idea. 'One obstacle removed at least!'

'More or less.' Lillian looked faintly perplexed. 'I must say, you're taking it all very calmly.'

'What do you expect, screaming hysterics?' It was almost on the tip of her tongue to blurt out the truth, but something stopped her. There were too many points unexplained—such as why Liam had not seen fit to acquaint Lillian with the truth himself, having realised what she still meant to him. Unless that part of it was simply Lillian's own version. She had got Liam here hoping to light old fires again, and had apparently succeeded up to a point. But was he really prepared to go beyond that point? Only Liam himself could answer that.

'I'm going in,' she said tautly. 'He can have his freedom any time he wants it.'

It is difficult to make a dignified exit wearing only a wet swimsuit and a towel. Jaime doubted if she succeeded. Had she possessed the means, she would have thrown her things back into her suitcase and left Liam to it. But she was stuck with the situation, like it or not. One thing she was sure of, though—she was not going to be party to what was going on between him and Lillian. The first opportunity she had she would tell him so.

CHAPTER SIX

IT wasn't far off lunchtime when she reached her room. She showered and changed into a print shirtwaister, descending the stairs to find the others down before her. Liam had changed into slacks and shirt; his hair was still damp at the ends from the shower. He was laughing and talking with Hal in a manner which made her want to accuse him right there and then of betraying the other man's trust. Lillian stood close by him, her arm brushing his as she lifted her glass, whether by accident or design it was difficult to tell.

'We're just clinching the deal,' said Hal, seeing Jaime in the doorway. 'Liam chose the sorrel.'

'I'd like both,' the other said, 'but he won't play.'

There was something uncomfortable in Hal's smile. 'Could be I might decide not to sell the bay after all. She doesn't have much in the way of form herself, but with her breeding, and mated right, she could still drop a good one.'

Lunch was not a pleasant meal, not for Jaime at least. There was too much of an atmosphere. Hal was quiet and introspective, seemingly unaware of the glances his wife kept bestowing on the man at her side. In actual fact, Liam himself seemed unaware of them too—or he was deliberately ignoring them. Jaime couldn't decide which.

There was no opportunity to talk to him alone during the rest of the day, nor when it came to it, the evening either. It was Hal who suggested eating out at the country club, leaving Jaime with the distinct impression that he needed the distraction. She wondered if it was regret over the sale of the sorrel that was eating him up, yet he hardly seemed the kind to let it show.

They were halfway through the evening before it occured to her that he too might be aware of his wife's covert little plans. Lillian believed she had persuaded him into selling to Liam because he owed him something, but wasn't it equally possible that he had sacrificed a principle in order to test her fidelity when it came to the man she might once have married instead of him? It didn't take much perception to see the difference in the way she was with Liam. They were dancing together now, two dark heads almost touching as Liam bent his to hear what was being whispered in his ear; two minds plotting—what?

'Hal,' she said, 'how long will it take to arrange shipping for the filly?'

He shrugged. 'A couple of days maybe. Depends how Liam intends going about it.'

'What's the best way?'

'Private charter from here to New York, I'd say, then scheduled freight through to Manchester.'

'That's going to cost a lot.'

'Daresay he can stand it. You're not marrying a poor man.' His tone was light but there was irony in the line of his mouth. 'Money has it uses.' He caught her eyes across the lamplit table and made a sudden contrite little gesture. 'Forgive me, that was tasteless.'

'But you think that's why I'm marrying him,' Jaime said quietly. 'For his money.'

He looked at her for a long moment, eyes revealing a complexity of emotions. 'I don't know what to think,' he said at last. 'You two don't act like any other engaged couple I ever saw. Once or twice I could have sworn you hated the guy.'

Once or twice had been more than right, she reflected grimly. Aloud she heard herself saying, 'And Liam? What would you say his motives were?'

'We're a different breed. We see what we want to see.'

'Or sometimes what you don't want to see?'

His gaze went from her face to the couple out on the dance floor, again, expression changing. 'Jaime, you don't know the half of it,' he said wearily.

'I know enough.' It seemed incongruous to be sitting here talking like this on little more than twenty-four hours' acquaintance, but what about this whole affair was normal? 'You're afraid of losing her, aren't you, Hal?'

He gave a harsh-sounding laugh. 'Afraid? You want to know the real reason I changed my mind about letting Liam have that filly? I hoped he might take her off my hands if he got the chance. I hadn't counted on you, of course.'

Jaime's mind felt blank. First one and now the other! Looking at him she thought: he's bluffing. There was pain behind the façade. She said steadily, 'I don't believe that. Neither do you.'

The air went out of him suddenly like a pricked balloon. For the first time the years showed. 'I wish I did,' he said. 'It surely would help.' He put out a large hand to take hers, covering it lightly. 'I never intended saying what I did just now. Guess I forgot myself. My troubles aren't yours.'

They are if Liam is involved, Jaime started to say, and stopped herself abruptly. Nothing he did concerned her. A week from now she would be free of him, perhaps even less than that if he got things moving. And he had better.

It was late when they got back to Rayburn. Both Jaime and Lillian refused a nightcap, leaving the two men to indulge themselves alone. Once in her room, Jaime prepared for bed swiftly, pulling on a loose wrap before settling down to wait until she heard Liam come up. This was likely to be the only opportunity she was going to have to get him alone, much as she hated the idea of going to his room. They had to talk—it was imperative. No way was she going to stand by and see Hal done down.

Almost an hour passed before she heard what she was waiting for, and even then she had to nerve herself to stick to her guns. She moved across the corridor softly, hesitating a further moment before tapping once on the door.

He seemed a long time answering the summons. When he did open up she saw he was already undressed and wearing a bathrobe, his hair tousled as if he had just run a hand through it. For a moment he just stood there looking at her, expression undergoing a subtle change.

'Who were you expecting?' she asked with a bravado donned for the occasion. 'Lillian?'

Mouth tightening, he reached out a swift hand and jerked her forward into the room, closing the door behind him and barring her exit. 'I don't know why you're here,' he said, 'but I'm not swapping innuendo out there.' His glance raked her, smile twisted. 'Prepared for another try? You don't give up easily.'

'Don't worry,' she retorted. 'I'm no more eager to have you near me again than you are. I just have one thing to say to you, that's all.' She paused and drew breath, fanning her anger in order to maintain her courage. 'You'd better arrange to have that filly shipped out of here very quickly if you don't want Hal to learn what's going on.'

He regarded her narrowly, hands thrust into the slit pockets either side of his robe. 'Mind telling me what's supposed to be going on?' he asked with deceptive quietness.

'You and Lillian.'

'Yes?'

She bit her lip, sensing ridicule. 'Don't try making out it never happened. Lillian told me a different story.'

'I'm sure she did.' He didn't move, but there was something in his stance that cautioned. 'Supposing you tell me it.'

'I might have expected you to deny it. It would have been a surprise if you'd admitted it!'

He said softly, 'If you don't stop declaiming and start explaining I'll give you the *shock* of your life, much less a surprise! What the hell am I supposed to have done?'

'This morning,' she said. 'When you were out riding. You ... she said you ... made love to her.'

'Did she now?' His tone was almost amused. 'How?'

Jaime gave him a disgusted look. 'You're not even bothered about it, are you? You don't give a damn for the way Hal might feel! Or do you get your kicks out of knowing it? Resentment lasts a long time when it's fostered by hurt pride!'

'The voice of experience?' He was looking at her with calculation. 'You know, I was right this morning, beating you wouldn't be a bad idea! At the very least it might knock some of the sheer bloody gall out of you!'

'It takes someone like you to resort to threats,' she came back with scorn.

He took a step towards her, then paused and shook his head. 'If I once got started I wouldn't know where to stop! You've been needing it for too long.' Eyes glinting, he added, 'And I have a better idea. Not your choice this time, but mine—and for different reasons.'

Jaime froze as he reached out for her. Backing, she

said, 'You touch me and I'll scream loud enough to bring the whole household in here! I'd like to see you try explaining *that* away!'

His laugh was derisive. 'You won't scream.'

He was right. She found herself incapable of uttering a sound as he lifted her bodily and carried her over to the bed. Laid down on the pillows, she felt the mattress tilt to his weight as he joined her, his body pinioning hers in a way which left little room for escape.

'I could have done this the other nights,' he murmured close by her ear, 'except that I object to being led by the nose!'

His teeth found her lobe, jerking a sudden gasp from between her clenched jaws. The sensation of his lips moving against her skin was exquisite, drawing an immediate and involuntary response she couldn't hide from him. She raked her nails down the back of his hand, twisting her head away from him.

'Leave me alone!'

'That's not what you want,' he said. 'I'm not blind—*or* insensitive. Come on, Jaime, let yourself go. It's what we both need.' He was talking softly, moving his mouth between each word to tantalise yet another portion of her throat and neck, finding the softness of her breasts as he eased away the covering material. 'We don't need this—it's in the way. I want to feel this lovely body of yours against me, warm and smooth, and pliant.' His hands curved her waist, their touch gentle yet demanding at one and the same time. 'Like silk. That's what you should wear if you wear anything! Black silk against white skin, moulding every line. Purity wrapped up in sensuality—that's exciting to a man.' He had brought his head up again to hers, seeking her mouth. 'Kiss me, the way you kissed me the other night.'

She did so because she couldn't stop herself, lips parting to his demand with a hunger she could not contain. At the back of her mind was the knowledge that later she was going to regret these moments, but for now desire held the upper hand. His robe had come open to the waist, held only by the tie belt about his middle. She could feel the hair on his chest against her skin, creating a tingle which swept deliciously through her whole body. She slid her fingers through it and along the width of his shoulders beneath the material of the robe, tracing the run of muscle under his skin. Arms strong enough to crush, yet gentle enough to hold her now without hurting.

'Liam ...' she whispered, and didn't know whether she said his name in pleading for him to stop or carry on. 'Liam...!'

They neither of them heard the door open softly, or the faint rustle of silk as someone slipped through it. It took Lillian's gasp to bring them both down to earth and back to reality. Jaime felt her face flame as she met the outraged blue eyes over Liam's shoulder.

Liam himself made no move after that one twist of his body to see who was there. His face looked carved from stone, his jaw clenched.

'What the hell do you think you're doing?' he clipped. 'Get out of here, Lillian. And I mean right now!'

She turned without a word and left, shutting the door again with scarcely a sound. Jaime came out of the suspended animation into which the interruption had thrown her to sudden quivering realisation.

'Oh God,' she said, and it was almost a sob. 'Get away from me!' The hands which bare moments ago had touched him with longing and need clenched into fists, thudding against his bare chest. 'Get away!'

He seized her wrists and held them still, pinning her back on the pillows. His face was set, his eyes like granite. 'Stop it!' he said. 'Just calm down!'

She almost spat the words at him. 'You damned lousy cheat! I wish you were a man—I'd kill you!'

'If you were a man you wouldn't be here in the first place,' he came back without humour. 'I didn't ask her to come, you little fool!'

'Liar!'

'I'm not lying!' He shook her by the wrists, fingers cutting into her skin. 'I tell you I didn't ask her to come!'

Jaime made a supreme effort to free herself, sinking back with a strangled little sob when she failed. 'Then why did she? Just tell me that!'

'Because she has the same superb vanity she always had, that's why.' His tone was harsh. 'A wink's as good as a nod to a blind man.'

She stared at him, forgetting to fight for a moment. 'What are you talking about?'

'Something that's none of your business. Just take it from me that I do know what I'm talking about. God knows, I should.'

'I don't believe you,' she said. 'You're making it up. You made love to the woman this morning, why not tonight too?'

'I kissed the woman this morning,' he said between his teeth. 'And only then because she made it practically impossible not to. Leave it, Jaime. I'm not going to explain any more. It doesn't have anything to do with you.'

'She saw us just now—that makes it very much something to do with me!' She drew a shuddering little breath. 'Let me up, Liam. You can hardly expect to keep me here now.'

'I don't expect anything.' The smile was faint. 'You

might say I lost the immediate urge. But you're not getting the chance to run to Hal with your version of what happened tonight either. I want your word on it.'

'Would it mean anything to you?'

'It had better. Do I have it?'

Jaime nodded, sitting up when he let her go to eye him with loathing, clutching her wrap to her. 'I wouldn't have told Hal anything. He's too nice to be hurt that way.'

'I agree. He has enough on his plate already.'

'He'd be better off divorcing her,' Jaime said fiercely. 'She doesn't have any feeling for him.'

'But he does for her, God help him. There's nothing more pathetic than a man so obsessed with a woman he can't see her for what she is.'

'Did you?' she asked. 'Four years ago, I mean. It's so easy to talk in retrospect.'

'I told you, I'm not prepared to discuss it.' He got up then, pulling the robe about him and tightening the belt with a rough gesture. 'You'd better get back to your own room.'

'I'd hardly want to stay here.' She slid off the bed and stood up unsteadily, avoiding his eyes. 'I don't want you near me again—any time!'

'I'll have you any time I want you,' he said on a hard note. 'Don't pull the self-righteous bit on me! You're about as incapable of saying no to a man as most men would be of refusing what you're offering. Not your fault, I suppose, some women are made that way. I might have passed it up the other night, but I shan't be doing it again, believe me. In fact, if you stick around much longer I'll put you on your back again right now!'

Jaime was as white as a ghost, every limb trembling. 'Even if I was the way you think I am,' she got out thickly, 'you'd have no right to speak to me like that!

All right, so I lost my head just now. It's hardly surprising—you've obviously had a lot of practice. If—if Lillian hadn't come in when she did, I daresay it would have been over by now. I didn't stand a chance against you, and you knew it.' Her voice was starting to break up little by little despite everything she could do to stop it. 'Only if we h-had carried on you might have been rather surprised. A man is supposed to be able to tell when he's the first, isn't he?'

The silence was long and tense. Liam was looking at her as though he had never really seen her before, eyes narrowed and piercing, face immobile. Then slowly the hardness faded, replaced by a look of rueful regret mingled with something else not merely as easy to read. He reached out and drew her to him again, hand suddenly gentle, holding her with his cheek resting against her hair. She heard his sigh.

'Jaime,' he said, 'I'm sorry. I've treated you badly. What can I say?'

'It's enough if you believe me.' Her voice was muffled against his shoulder. 'Just believe me, Liam.'

It was a moment before he said, 'Is it so important for me to believe you? To you, I mean?'

She could only be honest about it. 'Yes.'

'Why?'

'I ... don't know why.'

He held her a little way from him so that he could see her face, searching it with the same questioning look. 'On the rebound from Tris? It wouldn't be the first time that had happened. We've been together a lot since.'

'I don't know,' she said again. 'I honestly don't know what I feel, Liam. You ... make me hate you most of the time.'

'But not enough to stop you wanting me to make love to you,' on a curious note. 'You do, don't you, Jaime? You wanted it in New York.' His smile was wry. 'You damned nearly succeeded too.'

'Except you don't like being led by the nose.'

'That, and because I genuinely thought I was just the latest in a succession. A man likes to think he's a special case, not one of a crowd. And you don't exactly give the impression of being behind the door when it comes to response.'

'I'm twenty-four,' she said. 'And I'm not trying to say I've never wanted to make love with anyone before, just that it never got that far. The one man who might have broken down my defences never really tried.'

'Tris.' It was a statement, not a question. 'And we both know the reason why he never tried. I'm glad he had that much regard.' He paused, still studying her. 'How do you feel about him now?'

'Dead,' she confessed. 'There's just nothing there. Yet I did love him, Liam, I *know* I did!'

'I guess it's possible to fall out of love as quickly as in it. He certainly gave you cause enough.'

'It wasn't his fault.'

'Of course it was his fault! He should have had the guts to go after Susan long before instead of looking round for a substitute. It wasn't fair on you.'

'Perhaps not, but I can understand better now what he felt.' She stirred, not wanting to leave his arms but knowing she must. 'I'd better go.'

'Do you want to?' He spoke softly. 'If I asked you to go to bed with me now, would you?'

Her heart contracted. 'I'd want to,' she said with honesty. 'But it isn't enough, is it?'

'It was a few minutes ago.'

'Only because you didn't give me the chance to think straight.'

Liam smiled a little. 'Is that the only way I'm going to get to you?'

'No.' She looked back at him steadily, trying to read what was in his mind. 'Can't we just leave things the way they are for now and see what happens?'

'That's asking a lot.' He pulled her to him again, holding her close. 'I want you, Jaime. If you want me too why shouldn't we enjoy it?'

'I ... can't,' she whispered. 'Liam, please ...'

'Is it because of Lillian?'

It wasn't, not wholly, but she seized on it for want of any other explanation. 'She must have had *some* reason to believe you wanted her to come to you tonight.'

He was still for a moment, then he took her by the arms and put her away from him to look at her. 'You're making it a condition I tell you about her?'

'No, of course I'm not making it a condition. If you don't want to talk about it, you don't, and that's all there is to it. Anyway,' she added with more conviction than she actually felt, 'I still wouldn't be staying with you. I'm not equipped to handle an affair.'

'What are you afraid of?' His tone was gentle. 'It might not turn out to be just another affair. Let me tell you something, Jaime. Two years ago a girl caught my eye because she had something which drew me regardless of what she happened to be up to at the time—or what I believed she was up to, at any rate. When Tris brought you to Oakleigh I felt the attraction again without immediately connecting it with that time in Ashbourne. It made me even less ready to accept you as his fiancée. Then when I remembered ...' He broke off, shook his head. 'It was like a red rag to a bull. Even if Susan hadn't shown up I'd have broken you two up. Either that or I'd probably have surpassed myself by trying to seduce my future sister-in-law.'

Jaime was gazing at him like a child at a problem picture. 'You wouldn't.'

'I would,' he mocked. 'I'd have no more been able to keep my hands off you than I can now. There's something inevitable about all this, you know. We've come together again for a purpose. Do you believe in fate?'

Her lips firmed suddenly. 'I don't believe anything is inevitable. There's always a choice.'

'Then make it my way. Life's too short to hang around waiting to see what might develop. Who's to say we wouldn't move on to a lasting relationship from here? There's every chance.' His voice deepened persuasively. 'Jaime, I want to make love to you. Right now there's nothing I want more than that. Come to bed, and let tomorrow take care of itself.'

He kissed her again, long and lingeringly, lifting her up to him with hands that bruised. Jaime felt the fire rising in her, the aching need to be closer; to know the sheer relief of letting herself go with the tide. She kissed him back with a kind of hopelessness as he slid off her wrap, only pausing when he put his fingers beneath the shoulder straps of her nightdress to ease them over and down.

'Liam, I'm sorry,' she whispered. 'It's no use, I can't!' She put her hands quickly over his, staying the movement, hardly daring to look him in the face.

'For God's sake!' He was tight-lipped and blazing, gripping her so hard she cried out in pain. 'What kind of a game do you think you're playing? First you will, then you won't! What the hell am I supposed to be made of?'

'I know,' she said. 'And I'm sorry. I can't explain.'

Miserably she added, 'I wish I could forget about everything else like a man can. It just isn't me, that's all. Right now ...'

'Right now,' he interrupted grimly, 'I think I'd have every excuse for taking you.' He put his hand under her chin, bringing her head up so that she had to look at him. 'That would settle the whole thing, wouldn't it? Remove the guilt by taking away the choice. Is that what you want?'

'No!' She could hardly breathe, his fingers hard against her windpipe. 'I know there's nothing you can say I don't deserve, but it isn't an answer.'

'It could be for me. I'd make you ...' He broke off and let go of her abruptly, turning away from her. 'You'd better go while you can.'

Biting her lip, she said, 'Liam ...' in a pleading little voice, and saw his jaw contract with a sharpness that made the muscles of his neck stand out in relief.

'Jaime,' he said, 'if you don't get out of here I'm going to hurt you. Enough is enough!' He looked at her, and the anger went out of him suddenly, leaving him weary. 'Go on,' he said. 'Out. I'd have been better off settling for Lillian.'

'Even though you despise her?'

His lips twisted. 'When did I say that?'

'You didn't, not in so many words.' Jaime sought for the right ones herself. 'Perhaps it's wishful thinking on my part. She's not a person I can admire. Did you know she's planning on asking Hal for a divorce so she can marry you?'

His brows lifted. 'She told you that?'

'This morning. She seemed to think you wanted your freedom too, so I gathered you hadn't told her about us.'

'And immediately suspected you were here simply to lull Hal's suspicions, if he had any.' There was irony in his voice. 'Wrong guess. Admittedly I lied a bit regarding the reasons I did want you to come with me. It wasn't a buffer I needed, it was a safeguard. Do you think I didn't recognise her hand in Hal's offer to let me buy that filly? It isn't the first time she's tried to get me to come over here since her marriage. She just doesn't know when to call it a day, that's all.' The pause was brief. 'If you're not going will you put your robe on again. You're not helping by standing there like that.'

Jaime bent and retrieved the garment, slipping her arms back into the sleeves and fastening the belt about her waist with quick fingers, face flushing a little when she lifted it again. 'Sorry.'

'Yes,' he said, 'I know. So am I.' He moved to extract a cigarette from the case on the bedside table, lit it and looked across at her through the smoke as he put the lighter down again. 'So maybe you should hear the whole story. That will make three of us who know the truth. When I asked Lillian to marry me I knew I wasn't the first man in her life by a long chalk, but I was infatuated enough to think being the last would make up for a lot.' His smile was grim. 'It didn't work out. She couldn't leave any man alone—even Tris. He had to tell me about it in the end because it was getting him down, though he hated doing it. Anyway, that was all I needed to finish it. Unfortunately, Hal was staying at Oakleigh at the time, so I let it ride until after he'd left. Next thing I knew Hal was telling me they were going to get married while Lillian stood there with him daring me to say a word.' He paused a moment, eyeing the smouldering end of the cigarette with cynical expression. 'She knew I wouldn't. I doubt if he'd have believed me if I'd tried to tell him what she was. So here she is. On the face of it, I'd say she's led Hal one hell of a life this last four years. Knowing her, I could pick out the men she's slept with among that crowd last night. There's a certain air of possession in the way she looks at a man she's had.'

'Yes,' Jaime said softly, 'I've noticed.'

His shrug came without rancour. 'Anyway, there you have it. Obviously I didn't want to go into all that when I asked you to come with me, so I played on the pride theme. Thought that might strike a chord, seeing your own had just suffered a blow.'

'It did,' Jaime admitted. 'I actually thought I'd misjudged you.'

'Then there was the other motive,' he went on as if she hadn't spoken. The smile was faint. 'I don't seem to be getting very far with that either.'

'You mean you planned all along to get me into bed with you this trip?'

'Hoped,' he corrected. 'Seems I miscalculated.'

'Yes, you did.' Her throat hurt. 'All the way. What are you going to do about Lillian now?'

'Nothing. Short of rubbing Hal's nose even further in it, there's nothing I can do. With any luck, we'll be away in another couple of days.'

'I hope so.' She paused. 'I'm glad you told me about her. Personally, I think she needs help.'

'That, I'm afraid, is Hal's worry.' He reached out and stubbed the cigarette with abruptness, then looked back at her. 'Jaime, come here,' he said softly.

'No.' She pulled the wrap about her more firmly. 'Not again. I'm going back to my room now.'

'No strings,' he said. 'I promise.'

'I don't trust you.' She started moving towards the door, heart thudding when he moved in front of her and blocked her way. 'Liam, it's no use. I'm not going to change my mind.' There was an edge of desperation to her voice. 'Just let me pass.'

'I'm not going to try changing your mind. I just want to hold you for a moment or two, that's all.'

'It won't be all, and you know it,' she protested, but she made no move to avoid the arms reaching out for her, leaning her head against his shoulder. 'I told you I can't handle an affair.'

'Supposing we start from the beginning again,' he said. 'We've both been under a misapprehension.' He smiled. 'Who knows, we might even learn to like one another.'

'I don't see any point.' She was trying hard not to let his touch get to her. 'There can't be any future in it.'

'Why? Because of Tris?' There was a small silence, then he said, 'Let's cross that bridge if we come to it. All right?'

'All right.' She kept her tone neutral. When he kissed her she had to force herself not to respond too eagerly, aware that even now it wouldn't take much to make her give in.

If Liam recognised it too he made no attempt to follow it through, letting her go with a wry curve to his lips. 'See you tomorrow. It won't be a pleasant stay from now on—Lillian will see to that.'

'All this,' Jaime said with a catch in her voice, 'for a horse!'

'Something only another horse-lover would understand.' He moved away to open the door for her. 'Happy dreams.'

In bed at last some minutes later, she lay in the darkness trying to sort out her emotions. Liam could make her feel like no man had ever made her feel before, she could say that with certainty. But could that kind of feeling turn into anything deeper?

The answer stared her in the face. It could because it was already. She had known that since New York.

CHAPTER SEVEN

LILLIAN did not put in an appearance next morning. Hal apologised for her absence, saying she did not feel up to accompanying them to the racetrack. Sensing his underlying discomfiture, Jaime took the indisposition with a pinch of salt. It was far more likely that Lillian had flatly refused to go and left it to her husband to find a reasonable explanation. Her ego must have taken a severe jolt last night, yet she could hardly stay out of their way altogether for the rest of their time here at Rayburn. Or could she? Women like Lillian were a law unto themselves—and the house was certainly big enough.

Liam made no reference to the previous night's happenings, but there was a subtle difference in his attitude towards her that warmed Jaime's heart. Perhaps his regard for her was merely physical at present, but that could change given the right incentive. She resolutely shut out the small voice that asked what real future there could be in it for either of them. Her previous relationship with his brother was a hurdle too far ahead to worry about now.

One thing she did doubt was her ability to hold out against him next time he made love to her. And there would be a next time; he had made that plain enough. Having high-flown ideals was all right, she decided wryly, while there was no temptation to cast them aside. Last night had been difficult enough, heaven knew, when everything in her had wanted to let go. Twenty-four and still a virgin. Something to feel proud of, perhaps, yet in some obscure way almost an embarrassment. It all stemmed from one's upbringing, she supposed. She could remember her mother's oft-repeated if, at the time, somewhat limited warning: 'Boys don't respect girls who let them go too far'. But Liam was no boy, and she herself was no longer so young as to be ignorant of the consequences. She was falling in love with him, and this time with a depth of feeling she knew she had never experienced before. In those circumstances the word 'no' became a ritual almost impossible to observe.

They reached the track shortly before noon, and lunched in the members' restaurant before going down to watch the first race. Rebel Lad was running in the second. Jaime had ten dollars on him to win, laughing when Hal derided her conservatism.

'I'll be more than delighted with this at those odds,' she said, waving her ticket. 'I could win almost a hundred dollars!'

'Will,' Hal corrected with confidence. 'And you're only getting that price because we've managed to keep his trial times a closely guarded secret. Wasn't easy, I can tell you. Little enough to be done if some tout managed to clock him, except watch the price fall. As it is, they've been shortened some by his breeding. White Lady won just about everything worth winning in her day.'

Liam had backed the roan too, although for how much Jaime had no way of knowing. He seemed unconcerned as he studied the horses being led around the ring, comparing points with a practised eye.

'The bay over there—number five. Could be trouble,' he commented to no one in particular, and Hal gave him a shrewd glance.

'I might have expected that from you. Dancer's the

only real contender. But Rebel can take him over the distance.'

The jockeys were starting to come through, the colours of their silks dazzling in the afternoon sun. The Lessing colours were gold on orange, the wearer this afternoon a serious-countenanced, wiry little man whose age could have been anywhere between twenty-five and forty. Hal's trainer said a few words to him, then a bell rang and the instruction was given for the jockey's to mount.

They all watched the man legged up on to the roan and start out on the parade in alphabetical order before adjourning to the stands to watch the race run. Jaime found the whole process far more exciting than she had ever imagined. The crowds, the vivid scenery, the contained hubbub all about her combined into an atmosphere to which it was impossible not to react. She watched the field of ten horses canter slowly round to the starting stalls through a spare pair of racing glasses, hearing Hal's small sigh of relief at her side when the roan went in without any trouble.

The few seconds' waiting seemed interminable, then came a concerted cry echoing the 'Off' over the loudspeakers. At first there was just a blur of colour moving in a massed group along the back straight. It took the commentator to sort out one horse from another, voice rising in pitch as the field began to string out:

'Coming round the far turn now, and it's Dancer out in front with Easy Runner close behind followed by Moonshot and Rebel Lad coming up fast on the rails; running down the hill it's Dancer still pressed by Easy Runner and Rebel Lad coming up into third place as Moonshot drops back.'

'Hold him,' Hal was muttering, glasses clamped to eyes. 'Wait for the marker!'

'And it's Dancer half a length in front of Easy Runner and going strong; Dancer and Easy Runner followed by Rebel Lad still holding in well; and passing the furlong marker it's Dancer—and Rebel Lad overtaking Easy Runner on the rails; Rebel Lad drawing level with Dancer. Fifty yards to go and it's Rebel Lad and Dancer neck to neck; and Rebel Lad forging ahead—just watch that horse pull away: Rebel Lad clear by a length and passing the post. Rebel Lad with Dancer second and Easy Runner third.'

Jaime had barely been conscious of screaming out encouragement with the rest, only of the rising crescendo of excitement as the horses came thundering down the final straight. Without thinking about it she turned and flung her arms about Hal's neck in wild enthusiasm shouting, 'He did it! He did it!'

Hal made no attempt to disengage her, half laughing, half serious, as he swung her round. 'Only just! He nearly came too late. I told Benson to let him go on the marker not five yards after it! He's have won by three lengths if he'd gauged it right!'

'He won,' said Liam. 'That's the main thing.' He was smiling, but the eyes resting on Jaime's lit-up face were enigmatic. 'Which do you want to do, collect your winnings or see Rebel in?'

'She's coming to see him in,' Hal said. 'You both are!' He flung an arm about each pair of shoulders, urging them towards the steps. 'Come on, before they beat us to it!'

For Jaime the following moments were something of a blur. She was pushed and jostled in the crowd, drawn clear by Hal to enter the circle reserved for the winning horse and entourage and somehow found herself standing by the latter's side with his arm still about her shoulders and several people she recognised from a few nights ago pressing in about them showering congratulations. It wasn't until someone addressed her as Mrs Lessing that she realised not everyone in the vicinity was a close enough acquaintance of the family to appreciate the difference. Whoever it was had vanished among the throng before she could correct him.

Liam was standing a few feet away on the edge of the crowd. She felt her smile fade a little as she met the grey eyes and registered the look in them. He had heard too, of course, but that didn't explain the quality of his expression. It was barely her fault that someone had mistaken her for the absent Mrs Lessing. Obviously it was well known that Hal's wife was a great deal younger than himself.

They stayed for the following races, although Hal had nothing else racing that day. He was jubilant and expansive, swearing Jaime had brought him luck.

'I can't see what difference my being here made,' she protested laughingly. 'You were certain he was going to win anyway!'

'I was certain he was the best animal in the race,' he said, 'but it doesn't always follow.'

'And you wanted me to put my shirt on him,' she chided, borrowing the term lightly. 'Shame on you, Hal.'

His eyes twinkled. 'If he'd lost I'd have bought you another. Life isn't worth living unless you're prepared to take a chance now and then. Wouldn't you say so, Liam?'

Broad shoulders lifted. He didn't turn his head. 'Depends on the odds.' The pause was brief enough to be almost non-existent. 'I should have that charter fixed for the day after tomorrow, all being well.'

Hal looked his disappointment. 'I thought you'd at least stay out the week. Jaime, you're not ready to go yet, are you? It's her first trip over here. Three days was hardly worth coming for!'

Liam swung his head towards where Jaime stood, brow lifted. 'Want to stay on?'

It was unfair, Jaime thought, to put the onus on her that way. If she followed her instincts and said no it would sound as if she hadn't enjoyed Hal's hospitality. She compromised instead and said, 'Well, it would have been nice, but I realise you want to get the filly home as soon as possible.'

'Rubbish!' Hal exclaimed. 'She won't be in season for at least another month. Plenty of time.' He took her silence for agreement, clapping a hand on Liam's shoulders. 'That's settled then.'

Thinking of Lillian, Jaime regretted the fact. Staying on for Hal's sake was one thing, but there was still his wife to face again. After last night that couldn't be easy for any of them. She tried to catch Liam's eye, but he didn't look her way. There was a line to his mouth she didn't care for very much. Surely he wasn't blaming her for the change in his plans? If he was so keen to leave he should have stuck out for the day after tomorrow regardless.

It was gone five when they got back to Rayburn. Approaching it, Jaime thought again how beautiful the house looked standing on that slight rise. There had been some damage during the Civil War, Hal had told her, but the restoration had been so well undertaken that nothing showed. Two of the present staff were actually descended from slaves who had once worked on the plantation long before it was turned to its present usage. So far as Jaime could gather, both seemed proud of the association rather than resentful of its implication.

It was one of the latter who met them in the hall, his

normally cheerful countenance troubled as he handed a sealed envelope to Hal with a few low-toned words.

The way Hal stood looking at it for a moment before making any move to open it reminded Jaime of her own reactions the day Tristan had sent her that note via his brother: he knew what it was going to say. When he did rip open the envelope it was quickly, eyes scanning the few lines contained on the single sheet of paper and a blank, almost lost expression coming over his face.

'She's gone,' he said tonelessly. 'Lillian's left me.' His eyes went unseeingly from one to the other of his two guests, his body sagging as if in acknowledgement of defeat. 'Excuse me, will you. Some things I must do.'

Liam caught Jaime's arm as she made a small involuntary move to follow the older man. 'Leave him,' he said harshly. 'Sympathy's the last thing he needs right now.'

'I didn't really have anything in mind,' she confessed on a shaken note. She made a small helpless gesture. 'There's nothing much one *can* say, is there? What a horrible thing to happen!'

'It was bound to sooner or later. Hal knew it too.'

She gave him an oblique glance, taking in the hardness about mouth and jaw. 'You think last night had something to do with her deciding to make it sooner?'

'Maybe—though it would have been more in character for her to have found some way to get back at us both.' His lips twisted. 'Lillian won't be used to finding herself standing in line.'

'Don't!' Jaime's voice betrayed her hurt. 'You make it all sound so ... cheap!'

'Make it all sound so cheap?' Liam asked with soft inflection, and she flushed a little.

'You know what I mean. What happened last night was ...'

'Nothing happened last night. You held out, if you remember.'

She stared at him, uncertain of her ground. There was a glitter deep down in the grey eyes she didn't understand. She wanted to ask him what was wrong, but the words wouldn't come. Instead she said, 'Do you think he'll go after her?'

'Hal? I doubt it. I'd say there was a man who knows when he's had enough.' He eyed her for a moment. 'Maybe we should cut our stay short after all now this has happened.'

'Don't you think that might be worse for him in some ways?' she asked quickly. 'I mean, once the initial shock wears off he's going to need company to take him out of himself. At least ...'

'In that case we'd better stay and give it to him.' His tone was short. 'I'm going up to change. See you later.'

Jaime remained where she was, gazing after him with heavy heart as he moved towards the stairs. Obviously she had said the wrong thing, yet what else could she have said? To leave Hal flat at a time like this would not only be cruel but callous into the bargain. Surely Liam must realise their position when he thought about it?

If he had thought about it he gave little indication of it during the evening. Hal made every effort to appear in command of himself, conversing at random on a number of topics though excluding the personal. It was left to Jaime to do most of the responding as Liam seemed disinclined to talk very much at all. Throughout the evening she was aware of something in his attitude which put her on edge, although she couldn't have explained why.

By common if unspoken consent they all retired at eleven. Jaime had half hoped Liam would make some move towards renewing their relationship when they reached the door of her room, but all he said was, 'Goodnight.'

She nerved herself to say his name as he made to pass on, meeting the cool grey eyes when he turned back to look at her with a sense of confusion.

'Yes?' he said.

'Is ... anything wrong?' she forced herself to ask. 'Are you annoyed because I said we should stay on?'

There was irony in the slow tilt of his mouth. 'I'm tired,' he shrugged. 'It happens to the best of us. Ask me again tomorrow night and I might be ready to oblige.'

He was gone before she could form a reply. Not that there seemed much to say. They were back to square one, that was clear enough. Perhaps they had never really left it. That softening in his attitude she had sensed this morning could have been the product of her own desire to find it.

Supposing she had been right in her first assumption last night? she thought numbly. Supposing he had been expecting Lillian, and had seized on her own timely intervention to pay back the woman in her own coin for what she had done to him four years ago. With Lillian gone there was no reason now to ensure her further co-operation by pretending to believe in her. As to the physical side—well, that was something else. For a man it always was.

Sleep proved impossible. Admitting defeat after two hours or more of tossing and turning, Jaime switched on the bedside light again and sat up. There were hundreds of books in the library downstairs. Perhaps if she could interest herself in one of them she could put Liam where he belonged—right out of mind.

She pulled on a wrap and trod into slippers before leaving the room. The house was silent, an odd light left burning here and there to aid nightwalkers like herself in their passage. The library was on the far side of the hall. Jaime opened the door and reached out a hand to switch on a light, pausing in some consternation as the big wing chair over by the window swung towards her to reveal a figure sitting in it.

'Who's there?' Hal asked sharply, then his eyes, already accustomed to the darkness in which he had been sitting, supplied the answer. 'Jaime?'

'Yes,' she said. 'I'm sorry, Hal, I didn't realise anyone was in here. I ... just wanted a book.'

'You couldn't sleep?' His tone was dull. 'I couldn't either. Come and keep an old man company for a few minutes.'

She moved towards him softly, her own troubles forgotten in recognition of that cry for comfort, taking a seat on the padded window base in front of him as he swung the chair back again. He was wearing a monogrammed silk dressing gown over matching pyjamas, his feet clad in leather slippers.

'It's not true,' she said. 'You're not old enough to be old, Hal.'

'That's what she called me. Said she was tired of being married to an old man.' He sounded tired himself, and totally dispirited. 'She wants a divorce.'

It was difficult to know what to say. 'Have you any idea where she's gone?' Jaime asked at length.

He shook his head. 'Wouldn't be hard to have her traced. That's not the problem. She wouldn't come back if I went after her.'

'She might have to eventually.'

'For financial reasons, you mean?' His wry smile could be seen in the moonlight filtering in through the trees to the rear of the terrace. 'Unlikely. I settled a large sum on her some time ago, apart from her allowance. She's a wealthy woman in her own right, well able to live alone until our marriage is dissolved.'

'Does that mean you're going to divorce her?'

'It means I'm going to agree to a divorce. I doubt if Lillian would let me sue her, even if I wanted to.' He met Jaime's gaze with that same little smile touching his lips. 'I know I could find adequate evidence—I've not been blind so much as turning a blind eye these last years. I blamed myself that she needed other men, although there wasn't a great deal I could do about it. No matter how hard you fight it the hormones start decreasing, or changing—or whatever it is they do. I'm by no means impotent yet, but ...' He broke off, rubbing a hand over his chin. 'I'm sorry, I'm embarrassing you.'

'No, you're not.' Jaime said it quietly, sensing his slow disintegration and hating Lillian for the way she had done this thing. 'Hal, you're only fifty-nine ...'

'Nearly sixty.'

'All right, nearly sixty, then. So, I can see that things might start slowing down as you get older, but I'd imagine the mind adjusts too. It has to. Nature couldn't be that cruel!'

'I guess you're right about that.' He looked at her for a moment expression difficult to define. 'What you're really saying is I shouldn't have married a woman so much younger than myself.'

'Not entirely.' Jaime paused, then decided to be candid about it. 'I think what you did do was marry the wrong kind of younger woman—one who couldn't adjust her own needs.'

'And wouldn't even try because she didn't love me.' His hands were curved over the arms of the chair, his eyes closed. 'I should have found someone like you,

Jaime, someone with a capacity for understanding.' His mouth looked strangely vulnerable against the strong lines of his face. Do you think *you* could have loved a man thirty years older?'

Her movement forward to bend and put her lips gently to his was pure instinct: reassurance for a man whose confidence in himself was at its lowest ebb. She had not anticipated the reaction she got. Suddenly his arms were about her, pulling her down on to his knees, his lips returning the kiss with almost feverish intensity. She felt his fingers rake through her hair to hold her head in a cupped grasp, the beat of his heart against her breast, the whole vibrant personality of the man reaching out to envelop her.

She had barely begun to ease herself out of the embrace when the overhead lights snapped on with a suddenness that both startled and sickened her. Liam stood framed in the doorway, face set so hard she flinched just looking at it. He was wearing a dressing gown too; they seemed to play all their scenes in nightclothes, she thought with fleeting irony as she pressed herself to her feet.

Hal was the first to speak, expression distraught as he came upright. 'It isn't what it looks,' he said. 'Believe me, Liam! I ... guess I just lost my head.'

'You wouldn't be the first.' Liam still had a hand poised on the switch. He took it away, fist curling visibly as he let it swing to his side. 'When it comes to undermining principles there's no equal!'

'It wasn't Jaime's fault.'

'No? I didn't see her doing much struggling.'

'I tell you it wasn't like that.' Hal sounded desperate. 'For God's sake, man, try and understand. I was down here on my own, feeling pretty low, I can tell you, when

Jaime came in. I needed somebody to talk to. She lent me an ear, that's all. The rest just ... happened. Call it a straw for a drowning man, if you like.'

'I know exactly what to call it,' Liam said coldly. 'I'm not blaming you, Hal. My fiancée can be very persuasive when she sets her mind to it.'

'I'm not your fiancée!' It was out before Jaime had thought about it, jerked from her by Hal's wince at the use of the word. He was going through enough without believing that history was in the process of repeating itself. She faced up to Liam squarely, uncaring of the glinting anger in his eyes. 'Why don't you tell him the truth about us? The reason why you brought me out here with you.' She didn't wait for his reply, turning her head back to the older man standing in a stunned attitude at her side. 'I was a face-saver, that's all. Liam wanted that filly but didn't fancy having Lillian think he was unable to supplant her memory, so he asked me to play the part while we were here. So you see, you don't have to feel that what happened just now is going to make any difference to our relationship. In fact, it should have set his mind at rest by confirming a basic belief.'

Hal looked from one to the other of them with mixed emotions. 'Is that true?' he said finally to Liam.

'So far as it goes.' Recovery had been fast. Face expressionless, Liam added, 'It doesn't alter anything. I brought her here. I'm responsible for what she gets up to.' He looked at Jaime and visibly hardened again. 'What I've got to say to you I'll say in private.'

'If it's what I think it is you can take it as said,' she came back with a hard look of her own. 'Hal, I'm sorry you had to be involved in all this, but Liam believes I might have had some idea of trying to take over from

Lillian. Under the circumstances, I think you'll agree the sooner we leave the better.'

She moved towards the doorway, eyes defying Liam to stop her. He made no attempt, standing aside to let her pass him. Mounting the stairs she heard Hal saying something, then Liam answering, but was too far away to make out the words. The anger and pride which had carried her this far began to collapse, leaving her hurting. She was thankful to reach the sanctuary of her room. And she never did get that book, she realised. Not that it mattered. No amount of reading was going to take her mind off *this*.

CHAPTER EIGHT

SHE should have known Liam would not be content to leave it there, of course. He came in without bothering to knock some minutes later as she lay gazing at the ceiling trying to work things out in her mind. She was too nerveless to move when he came over to the bed to switch on the one lamp, looking at him with eyes gone wide and dark.

'What do you want?' she got out.

'The truth.' He sat down on the edge of the mattress and took her chin in his hand, turning her face into the light and studying it grimly. 'Did you know Hal was downstairs when you went down?'

Resentment surged through her. She jerked her chin free, but couldn't sit up because of his weight on the bedclothes. 'You know,' she said tautly. 'I'm *sick* of these suspicions of yours! Think what you like, Liam—I'm past caring either way! And take that ring with you when you go, I don't need to wear it any longer.'

'Answer me!'

'No.' Her tone was flat. 'I don't owe you any explanations. I don't owe you anything. I did what I was brought here to do.'

'No, you didn't,' he said dangerously. 'Not at all. I said I planned to get you into bed this trip, and here you are.'

'Not with you!'

'That can be remedied.' He stood up and took off his dressing-gown, flinging it over the foot of the bed. He was wearing only the bottom half of a pair of pyjamas, the hair of his chest extending down to the waistband. Jaime tried to get up as he lifted the cover, but he was too quick for her, sliding into the bed and pulling her down again into his arms.

Fighting him was not only futile, it would be inflammatory, Jaime told herself. In this mood it was what he wanted. She forced herself to lie perfectly still as he found her mouth with his, stamping down the immediate and involuntary response that flooded through her. No matter what he did she wouldn't move, wouldn't protest; wouldn't give him any encouragement at all. But it wasn't easy.

It was some time before Liam finally admitted defeat, rolling away from her with a stifled exclamation. For another moment or two he lay on his back looking up at the ceiling, then he gave vent to a short dry laugh.

'The original Iron Maiden,' he said. 'I'll say one thing for you, you've a will second to none!'

Jaime let out her breath on a shallow sigh, tension relaxing a little. If he'd carried on another minute she would have been lost.

'I won't be used,' she said. 'Now will you please get out of here.'

He propped himself up on one elbow to look at her. 'Why not?' he asked hardily. 'It works both ways. Some responses you can't hide.'

'Hard to fool an expert.' She was close to tears. 'Just go, will you, Liam.'

He didn't move. When he spoke again his tone was different, almost an appeal. 'All it takes is a word. Tell me you don't have any interest in Hal and I'll believe you.'

'For how long? Till something else happened to arouse

your lousy suspicions? Sorry, but I couldn't take that kind of uncertainty.'

'Any more than I could take another Lillian,' he came back roughly. 'I came across here earlier because I wanted to try talking things out. Instead I find you making up to Hal for all he's going to be missing with his wife gone—at least, that's how it looked from where I was standing. If there's some other explanation I'd be only too ready to hear it.'

'If I told you, you wouldn't understand it.' Jaime threw back the covers and found the floor with her feet, reaching for her wrap as she stood upright. 'You don't have what it takes to understand what Hal is going through,' she tossed over her shoulder. 'All you see is a man whose wife has left him. You probably even think he's well rid of her.'

'Yes, I do.' Liam was sitting up in the bed now, an arm about his bent knees. 'To use an outdated term, he's been made a cuckold long enough.'

'He knew that, and accepted it. Apart from throwing her out, how does a man stop his wife from making a fool of him?' She caught the quality in his silence, and shrugged. 'That wouldn't work with a woman like Lillian, and you know it. You knew it four years ago. Anyway, Hal isn't the type to throw his weight around.'

'You seem to have gleaned one hell of a lot about him in a few days.'

'Maybe I'm sensitive that way. I have to have *some* redeeming quality.' She supported herself with a hand against one of the lower bedposts, looking at him with blurred vision. Throat tight, she added, 'Are you going to stay there all night?'

'Not unless you're willing to come back and join me.'

'Disregarding everything else, of course.' Jaime shook

her head. 'You might be able to shut it out, but I couldn't. You don't trust me any way at all.' She gave a bitter little laugh. 'I wonder what it is that makes men think they have a right to past affairs and a woman doesn't!'

'I never said that. It's lies and subterfuge most of us can't take.'

'I always thought the basis of British justice was innocent until proved guilty? Circumstantial evidence doesn't constitute proof.'

'It constitutes reasonable doubt.'

'And that's enough for you to convict.'

'It's enough for me to have reasonable doubt.' He got up, reaching for his dressing gown but not bothering to put it on. 'I suppose you're right. Better to forget the whole thing. Thirty-six hours and we'll be on our way.'

'Can't I go tomorrow?' she asked woodenly. 'There's no need for me to wait for the charter.'

The pause was brief, his shrug when it came indifferent. 'No need at all. I'll phone the airport in the morning and try to get you on the afternoon flight. That suit you?'

'Fine.' There was a hard lump in her throat which made swallowing difficult. 'I'd like to get some sleep now.'

'Sure,' he said with irony, and moved towards the door. 'Pleasant dreams.'

So that was that, Jaime thought painfully when the door was closed. Episode over. Had she acceded to his demands a few minutes ago she would still have been in his arms right now, yet would it have made any difference in the long run? At least this way she retained her self-respect, if precious little else.

Hal was gruffly apologetic when they met next morning. Jaime had the feeling he was secretly relieved when she announced her intention of leaving that afternoon if possible, although he made the usual polite sounds of protestation. He had revealed too much of his inner self to her in those unguarded moments last night, she realised. Now he was battening down the hatches for a long lone voyage.

With her seat booked on the four o'clock flight to New York and her packing completed, there remained little to do after breakfast but hang around waiting for lunch and then departure. Jaime took a stroll through the formal gardens at the rear of the house, contemplated a swim, then abandoned the idea as it would mean packing a wet swimsuit for the journey, and returned indoors feeling that time was deliberately standing still.

One of the servants was on the telephone when she went out through the hall to reach the stairs. 'Mr Caine is down at the stud, suh,' he was saying in the soft Southern drawl which characterised all the staff at Rayburn. Then he caught sight of Jaime and his expression lightened. 'But his fiancée, Miss Douglas, is right here now!'

'Who is it?' Jaime mouthed as she took the receiver from him, and received a sickening jolt when he said blithely, 'Mr Caine's brother phoning from England, miss. It's sure a mighty clear line!'

It was—too clear. Tristan's voice came through like a bell, the disconcertion and utter confusion bridging thousands of miles. 'Jaime? What the devil is going on?'

In the few seconds' grace while he fired the obvious questions, Jaime thought of and rejected half a dozen answers. All she could find to say was, 'Liam asked me to come.'

'I gathered that.' He paused, obviously waiting for her to add something to the bare statement. When she didn't he came on again, voice more perplexed than ever. 'Jaime, he called you Liam's fiancée. Is that true?'

It was on the tip of her tongue to deny it, then she thought of all the explanations that was going to involve and paused irresolutely. How did she start explaining an arrangement such as theirs had been—or the motivations which had prompted her to accept at the time? Strange how truth could so often sound more implausible than fiction. When she did speak it was almost by instinct, the words forming themselves.

'I'm not all that sure at the moment, Tris. I don't suppose it stood all that much chance of working out considering the circumstances. Even if Liam had waited to ask me the situation would have been the same.'

The silence was lengthy. Jaime could hear all the other tiny sounds on the wire, sizzling and humming like bees round a far-off jampot. She could sense the thoughts racing through Tristan's mind and sympathised with his inevitable reactions. Too late to back out now; she had to go through with it.

'Let me get this straight,' he said at last. 'Liam asked you to marry him after we ... broke it off, and you accepted on the rebound. Is that what you're trying to say?'

'More or less.' She felt a complete fraud. She added thickly, 'Don't think too badly of me.'

'I don't.' His voice was unexpectedly gentle, rising again a little as he went on, 'I just can't imagine why Liam didn't tell me how he felt about you, if that was the case.'

'He thought it might create awkwardness.' She was improvising as she went along, sinking deeper and deeper into the mire. 'We were going to keep it quiet for a time until you and Susan were married.' She said the word without a quiver.

'I see.' He was quiet for a moment, breathing clearly audible. 'And it isn't working out, you say?'

'No.' That, at least, was the truth. 'It's my own fault.'

'Because you don't love him?'

'I suppose so.'

'It isn't your fault,' he said with rueful inflection. 'It's mine. All of it!'

'No, Tris!' Jaime was dismayed. 'No, you mustn't think that. I'm only sorry you had to know about it at all. And you're certainly not to let it concern you.'

'It has to concern me. Unfortunately, there doesn't seem to be a great deal I can do except leave the two of you to decide for yourselves. You could do a lot worse than marry Liam, Jaime. As to not loving him—well, there must have been some attraction there for you to even contemplate it.'

She said huskily, 'You mean you wouldn't object to having me for a sister-in-law?'

'Object? I'd be only too delighted! So would Susan.' The laugh was forced. 'It would relieve a considerable amount of guilt on both our parts.'

Jaime mentally shook herself. What was the use? No way was Liam ever going to marry her. 'Tris,' she said, 'why did you telephone in the first place?'

'Good God, I almost forgot!' His tone had changed completely. 'It's the stud. There's some kind of viral infection attacking the foals—newborn and yearlings. Brian Jacobs rang me an hour or so ago to say they'd lost the second one in thirty-six hours. I don't know that there's anything Liam could do if he were there at Oakleigh, but I didn't want him left in the dark about it. Will you tell him?'

'Oh, lord, how awful!' Jaime was distressed at the news. 'Yes, of course I'll tell him. As a matter of fact, he has a charter booked for tomorrow to New York. With any luck he should be home early Saturday morning.'

'Good. I'm going up tonight myself. You'll be coming with him?'

'To Oakleigh?' She hesitated. 'I don't think so. I must go and find Liam now, Tris. Goodbye.'

She put down the receiver with nerveless fingers. Whether she had done the right thing or not she had no way of knowing. At the moment she didn't even want to consider the alternatives. First she must tell Liam the bad news, and then there was her plane to catch. Lunch she discounted; eating at a time like this was out of the question.

She could have contacted Liam at the stud via the internal telephone, but she decided to wait his return instead. Whether he knew now or later made little difference. He could hardly leave before tomorrow without cancelling all his arrangements for the filly he had bought.

There was no sign of Hal, nor had been since breakfast. Jaime wandered disconsolately around the ground floor rooms, browsed for a while in the library regardless of the scene which had been enacted there the previous night, and emerged again into the hall the moment she heard Liam's familiar footsteps on the polished tiles.

'I'm afraid I've some bad news for you,' she announced without preamble. 'There's a viral infection at the stud, and they've lost two foals. I said you'd be home Saturday morning.'

The strong mouth had straightened abruptly. 'Why wasn't I contacted when the call came through? I assume it was a call?'

'Yes.' Jaime paused, then shrugged. 'There didn't seem much you could do from here.'

'How the hell would you know? At the very least, I could have got more details!'

'The call didn't come from Oakleigh. Brian contacted Tris in London.'

'Tris?' Grey eyes narrowed. 'You spoke to him yourself?'

'Yes.' This was the moment she had been dreading—the moment when any alternative seemed preferable to the one she had used. 'It was unavoidable. Benjamin put me on the line before I could do anything about it.'

'And?'

The door jamb was close against her back. She rested it there, hands behind her, meeting his gaze without flinching. 'He announced me as your fiancée. I had to think fast, and perhaps I didn't think straight.'

'What did you tell him?' Liam brought the words out with clipped precision. 'Just give me *that* straight, if you can!'

Jaime did, as well as she was able, watching his face darken. 'I could hardly tell him the truth,' she finished with a flash of spirit. ' "Your brother got me here in the hope of enjoying a short but lively affair"—do you think that would have sounded better?'

'It would have been closer to reality—except that you'd have had a hard time explaining away *your* reasons for accepting the offer in any good light.' He was taut and angry. 'You thought fast all right. Pity it's going to be wasted.'

'What are you going to do?' she asked as he moved towards the telephone table beneath the curve of the staircase. At that moment she could hardly bring herself to care.

'First,' he said, lifting the receiver and dialling, 'I'm going to get myself a seat on that plane this afternoon, then put a call through to Oakleigh to find out what I can—providing the delay isn't too long.'

'But the filly?' she said. 'You've arranged transport for the filly tomorrow.'

'Which still holds good. I'll just have to trust the ground staff both ends and arrange for a box to be waiting at Manchester airport Saturday morning.' He got through on his call, spoke rapidly and succinctly for a brief moment, paused while the position was checked at the other end, and then nodded his satisfaction. 'Thanks.'

'If you're going to be on that plane,' Jaime said, 'I'd rather not.'

'You'd prefer to stay on here and keep Hal company, I suppose.' He shook his head, mouth grim. 'We're both going to be on that plane this afternoon—and the flight from New York, as you heard. And don't think you'll be leaving me at Heathrow, because you won't. You're going to come on down to Oakleigh and tell Tris the truth this weekend if I have to tie you up to get you there!'

Hal found the opportunity to speak with Jaime alone before they left, his manner uncomfortable.

'I'm sorry,' he said, 'if I've caused trouble between you and Liam. That was the last thing I wanted.'

'I know.' Her tone was gentle. 'And you didn't cause anything that wasn't already there, Hal. There never was any love lost between us.'

'That's a pity,' he said, 'because you're well suited. Man like Liam needs a woman who'll stand up to him. Walk all over her otherwise.'

Jaime didn't need that pointing out to her; she was only too well aware of it. 'He won't have the opportunity,' she said. 'Goodbye, Hal. And I'm sorry—about everything.'

His smile was wry. 'Might be for the best in the long

run. Peace of mind only comes at cost. Take care of yourself, Jaime.'

Liam said little on the flight to New York. Jaime wondered if he intended maintaining the same cold indifference all the way across the Atlantic. The thought of what she faced at Oakleigh was hardly pleasant, yet she knew she had no choice but to go through with it. There had been a three-hour delay on the call Liam had tried to put through, so he had been forced to abandon the attempt. Whatever explanations she made to Tris they would have to start from scratch and could hardly show her in any good light. She doubted his ability to understand the lies she had told him over the phone.

They were due out of Kennedy at eight-thirty. Seated in the first class departure lounge waiting for the call to board, Jaime swiftly downed the gin and tonic Liam had ordered for her and asked for another, thinking wryly of what he had once said about alcohol dulling the edges.

'Trying to drink the bar dry?' he asked sotto voce when the second glass went the way of the first in an even shorter time.

'That's right,' Jaime answered, and was surprised to hear how clear and precise her voice sounded considering the way her head was starting to feel. 'I think I'll switch to something else for the next.'

Liam took the empty glass from her and pushed it to the far side of the table. 'You can drink yourself into a stupor once we're on that plane and you're strapped into your seat,' he said, 'but I'm damned if I'm going to carry you across the tarmac!'

'Too undignified,' she mocked. 'They might even take us for pop stars! I think I'm qualified to know my own limits, thanks.'

He caught her hand as she made to signal to the duty

steward, pressing it down between the two of them on the padded seat. His face was hard. 'I mean it, Jaime. You want a scene, you can have it, but you're not having anything else right now!'

She conceded defeat, knowing herself incapable of defying that glint in his eyes. The call to board came as a face-saver, enabling her to avoid his gaze as she gathered her things together. Alcohol might dull the reflexes, but it heightened the emotions. She had never wanted him as desperately as she did at that moment.

At altitude the spirit already in her bloodstream increased its effects to an alarming degree. Jaime fought down the waves of nausea, hoping they wouldn't be hitting any air pockets while this feeling lasted and wishing Liam had decided to take the heavy hand earlier than he had. Dinner she could not bring herself to look at, sending it back untouched. Liam made no comment, but she could sense the contempt in his occasional glance her way. Probably he thought it served her right to suffer a little after all he imagined she had done.

Eventually, worn out, she slept, awakening to the early morning stirring of cabin crew and passengers around her. Her mouth felt like a desert, but at least her head was clear again. She turned it as Liam settled himself back into the seat beside her, and hooked forward his flight bag with a foot. He had washed and shaved already, and donned a clean shirt from the look of it. Conscious of her own tousled, perspiration-darkened locks, Jaime wanted to crawl out of sight under the seat before he saw her.

'There's nobody in there at the moment,' he said as if reading her thoughts. 'You'll feel a whole lot better for a wash and brush-up.'

Jaime found her toilet bag without a word and stood

up to push past him, nerves tensing to the light touch of his hands on her hips as he eased her between his swivelled knees and the back of the seat in front. Locked within the toilet compartment, she shuddered at the sight of her pale features and lack-lustre hair in the mirror. It took her ten minutes to make any real improvement in her appearance, and even then she felt it left a lot to be desired.

'You're a fool,' she told herself in bitter derision. 'It isn't going to make the slightest difference *what* you look like!'

Liam watched her coming back to her seat with enigmatic eyes. This time he stood up to let her pass.

'Feel like breakfast?' he asked. 'They're starting to bring it round now.'

Jaime discovered she was ravenous thinking about it. Sitting down, she began tentatively, 'Liam ...'

'If you're going to say what I think you're going to say, the answer is no,' he interrupted smoothly. 'You're coming on to Oakleigh with me by hook or by crook. I want this thing straightened out once and for all.'

'You started it,' she pointed out. 'If you'd left me alone there wouldn't be anything to straighten.'

'I don't want to discuss it,' he said, man-like, and treated the stewardess to a smile Jaime would have given her eye teeth for. 'We'll both have the full English Country House, please.'

CHAPTER NINE

THERE were opportunities after they landed to lose herself in the crowds at Heathrow, of course. Standing about outside the main doors while Liam fetched the car round, Jaime contemplated making a run for it right here and now, but couldn't find the will. The only place to go was the flat, and he could easily find her there.

Once in the car and moving out of the airport area, she felt reconciled to the inevitable. With any luck she could be back in London by tonight. There would be little point in hanging around once Tristan had been told the truth. She only hoped she could keep from him—from them all—how she really felt about Liam. Better to have them regard her as he did than suffer that final indignity.

They made good time once they reached the motorway. By midday they were approaching the estate and Jaime's heart was as low as it could get. Seen in profile via the occasional stolen glance, his face looked unrelenting. He was so totally male, she thought, letting her eyes wander briefly but yearningly down over the broad shoulders and along his arms to the strong brown hands. Where would she ever find another man who could rouse her the way he could? If it came to that, would she ever be able to let another man touch her without longing for Liam's caresses, for his strength—even for his bullying? She had said once that he would want to dominate a woman far too much, but it wasn't strictly true. He would always be the boss, keeping her in line, demanding her respect, but he would know how to love her the way a woman wanted to be loved, and that was dominance of a different kind.

'What do we say to Tris?' she asked as the wrought iron gates hove into view. Her voice sounded a little desperate. 'Where do we start?'

'With plain brutal fact,' he came back, unmoved. 'I needed a woman and you wanted a man. He'll probably blame himself for leaving you unsatisfied.'

Her chin lifted. 'If a man was all I wanted why have I gone to such pains to deny myself the pleasure?'

'Because you've been playing for higher stakes—hence the tale you told him over the phone.'

'If I'm going to tell the truth,' she said, 'it's going to *be* the truth. I never wanted to marry you. I'm not that masochistic! You'd make life hell on earth for any woman!'

'But heaven in bed,' he said with a quirk of his lips. 'That much we could still salvage if we had a mind.'

They were drawing up in front of the house. Jaime said huskily, 'Your mind and mine are poles apart, and that's the way they're staying. After this, I don't care if I never see you or hear of you again!'

She was out of the car before he could move, standing for a moment in the bright sunshine to look at the man framed in the big oak doorway. It was a bit like going back in time—except that the positions had been reversed. Tristan's smile held an element of uncertainty.

'We weren't expecting you until morning,' he said as he came forward. 'Why didn't you let us know you were on your way?'

Liam closed his door with a short sharp slam and came round the car. 'Not much point considering there's only twenty-four hours' difference. How are things going?'

His brother pulled a face. 'Not good. The vet's down

with Brian now, but they haven't broken it yet. What happened to the filly?'

'With any luck she's on her way.' Liam paused for a brief moment, then turned back to the car. 'I'm going down to the stud. Take Jaime inside and give her a drink. I think she needs it.'

It was on the tip of her tongue to ask to go with him, but she knew it was useless. If he wanted anyone down there it certainly wasn't her. The fluctuating state of her emotions sickened her. Why couldn't she make up her mind and stick to it?

Tris took her indoors in silence. He didn't seem to know what to say to her. Jaime declined the drink Liam had suggested, knowing why he had suggested it. She needed more than dutch courage to start telling Tris what she had to tell him. She needed the right opportunity, for one thing, and this certainly wasn't it.

'Afraid it'll be a makeshift lunch,' he said apologetically. 'We've been making do on sandwiches these last couple of days or so. I just popped back to get them, seeing everybody else is busy.'

'How bad is it?' she asked. 'Did you lose any more foals?'

He shook his head. 'Not yet, but there's one almost certain. Funny, isn't it, how Liam never got round to naming that colt. He was the first to go.'

'Oh, Tris, I'm sorry.' Jaime was distressed. 'I wish there was something I could do.'

'There's nothing anybody can do that isn't already being done. So far there's been no response to any of the known serums. Harstead brought in a new experimental one this morning. He's trying it out now, although it could as easily kill as cure. We won't know for several hours.'

'Don't let me keep you if you want to get back.'

'I'd as soon not just yet. I'm no horse man, and I just get in the way. I'll take them down some food in a bit.' He paused and looked at her, the hesitation plain on his face. 'Jaime ...'

'There's plenty of time to talk about that, isn't there?' she appealed, and made a sudden decision of her own. 'Wait until Liam is here. He'll tell you all there is to be told. It's a bit complicated.'

'Not so much from where I stand. I can see how it might have happened. I should have realised when Liam offered to post that letter for me.' There was another pause. 'Is it still not going right?'

She shook her head. 'I'm only here because Liam made me come.'

'To sort things out?'

'You might say that.' She was being deliberately uncommunicative and she knew Tris recognised it, but couldn't bring herself to sail into explanations now. 'Do you think I might go and lie down? I feel shattered.'

'Oh, Lord, of course, you've been travelling all night. I think Pax prepared the same room you had last time. I wasn't sure whether or not you'd be coming, so I played safe.'

Jaime said painfully, 'Does Mrs Paxton know ... why I'm here?'

'Enough to put two and two together, I suppose.'

'And Susan?'

He flushed. 'Well, of course I had to tell her. She was a bit taken aback, but she says she can understand now why Liam turned so suddenly sympathetic to her cause after he'd seen you and realised he fancied you himself. Apparently he gave her a bad time the day she arrived home—told her we neither of us deserved any help in getting together again.'

Jaime looked back at him curiously, wondering at her total lack of emotion where he was concerned. 'Would you really have gone through with marrying me, Tris, if I hadn't walked out?'

He looked uncomfortable. 'I ... don't suppose so. I'd have found it difficult, though, because I really did feel something for you, Jaime, believe me.'

'Not enough for marriage,' she said, 'any more than it was on my part. We were two people looking for someone to love. You as a substitute for Susan; me because I'd never found anyone else I came even near to it with. There was no real need for each other there, and I think we both knew it.'

He made no attempt to deny it. Instead he said softly, 'Was it different with Liam?'

'Very.' Her throat closed up. 'The same room, did you say?'

'Yes.' Whatever his thoughts he didn't try to detain her further. 'I'll call you for tea.'

'Thanks. I just hope this serum works.'

She found her own way to the bedroom without seeing anyone. Her suitcase was still in the car, she realised. Not that it mattered. She had all she might need in her handbag—including aspirin.

She took a couple with a glass of water from the bathroom, then lay down on the bed after stripping off her suit jacket. The window was open to the warm afternoon. Difficult to realise it was only two short weeks since her last visit here. Two weeks to fall out of love with one man and in love with his brother! Except that what she had said downstairs was true—she had never loved Tris with this same desperation, this longing, this need to belong both physically and emotionally to one other person.

The sun had gone round the corner of the house when she awoke, dimming the room to a pleasant dullness. It wasn't until she lifted her head to look at her watch that she realised she was not alone. Liam stood over by the window, his breadth contributing to the lack of light. He turned when he heard the slight movement of the mattress springs, expression difficult to assess with his back to the available light.

'Had a good sleep?' he asked.

'I must have.' She came to a sitting position, memory coming back in a rush. 'The foals ...'

'The third one died an hour ago, but the new serum seems to be holding its own with the others.' He spoke without emotion. 'I gather you didn't get round to talking to Tris yet.'

'We talked, but not about that.' Jaime paused before adding hardily. 'When it came to the point I decided it ought to come from you if anybody. You can tell him everything at one go—how you first saw me that time in Ashbourne, and why you really asked me to go with you to Rayburn. You can even tell him how hard I tried to get you into bed in New York, and how noble you were in refusing. He won't understand because he never saw that side of me, but he'll believe it because you're his brother—and big brother never made a mistake in his life, did he?'

'Enough to be wary of making another. I thought I could change Lillian and found I was wrong.'

'I'm *not* Lillian!'

His lips firmed. 'All right, so prove it.'

'How?'

'You said it yourself not so very long ago. A man can tell when he's first.'

Jaime stared at him unmoving. 'You mean ... now?' she got out.

'Why not?'

'All women are born actresses,' she reminded him

scathingly. 'How do you know I couldn't act *that* part too?'

'Forewarned is forearmed.' The smile didn't reach his eyes. 'I'm not a fool.'

'Just a self-ordained expert on virginity!' Her voice was low and impassioned. 'Get out,' she choked, 'and don't bother coming back! I don't have to prove anything to you—or to anybody else either.' She stood up, albeit not very steadily. 'Tell Tris what you like. I'm going to be on that evening train.'

'How, by Shanks' pony?' He shook his head, mouth uncompromising. 'You're staying right here till I'm through with you. One way or another I'm going to get the truth.'

'Then make it another. I don't want you near me.'

'Liar,' he said, coming towards her. 'And don't bother trying to freeze me off, because it won't work this time.'

Pride kept her still as he pulled her into his arms, but it couldn't disguise the racing of her pulses nor conceal the inevitable response of her body to his touch. His mouth was demanding, leaving little room for refusal. She felt the desire rising in her, sharp and swift, the reticence fading before the stronger urge to follow his lead.

His hands moved down over her hips, lifting her to him, his own arousal a spur to the need racing through her. She found the buttons of his shirt and undid them, her hands sliding inside to the warmth of his skin. Bending her head, she pressed her lips into the dark curl of hair on his chest, scoring a passage through it with the tip of her tongue to the tune of his sharpened breathing and exulting in her sudden ability to let instinct guide her. With Liam there was no restriction, no restraint. She wanted to give him the same pleasure he was giving her, and know she was doing it.

He slid off her blouse and tossed it lightly on to the

bed behind her, mouth curving as he traced the line of the brief white brassiere she was wearing down to its centre join. 'You don't need this,' he said, and took it off, catching his breath as he looked at her, hands coming up to cup and mould. 'God, you're lovely! Venus with arms.'

She quivered to his touch, body arching closer, her hands going up and around his neck. 'Liam ...' she whispered.

'Jaime ...' he mocked, but there was no real bite in it. He found the fastening of her skirt and unclipped it, pausing with his fingers on the zip as he felt her tense a little, eyes questioning, 'Yes?' he asked softly.

It was too late to back out now. Too late—and beyond her. She pressed her face into his chest with a muffled sound.

The knock on the door was a shock her system could barely sustain. She froze in his grasp, mind not functioning fast enough to put words into her mouth in time. She heard the door open, but with her back to it had no idea who was coming in. Liam held her where she was, jaw clenching as he looked across her shoulder at the intruder.

'Next time wait till you're bloody well invited!' he clipped. 'What the hell do you want?'

'Sorry,' His brother's voice sounded shaken with embarrassment. 'I didn't realise ...' He broke off abruptly and pulled the door to again, murmuring something about tea being ready just before it closed.

Jaime pushed herself away from Liam in one jerky movement, turning her back on him as she reached for her blouse, fingers trembling almost too much to fasten the buttons when she had it on again. She felt cheapened, degraded; the memory of Tristan's gasp burned into her brain.

Liam hadn't moved, but she could feel him watching her. When he spoke it was wryly.

'My fault,' he said. 'I should have locked the damned door. Twice is one time too many.'

A shudder ran through her. 'You had it planned, didn't you?' she muttered. 'You came up here just for ... that!'

'If that, as you call it, was all I'd come for I'd have woken you right away instead of waiting. You talked yourself into it.'

'Really!'

'Yes, really.' Irony tinged his voice. 'I came up to tell you I'd changed my mind about telling Tris everything. He has such a touching faith in you I couldn't bring myself to destroy it.'

'Thanks.' She made herself turn and face him, meeting his eyes with a flush staining her cheeks. 'So where do we go from here?'

Liam's mouth twisted. 'For the time being it seems nowhere. We play the game through the way we've made it appear, that's all.'

'I can't,' she said on an edge of desperation. 'I can't face Tris again after him seeing ... What will he think?'

'That it's a good damned job he didn't barge in a few minutes later,' he came back brutally. 'He might not have shown it so much with you, but he's hardly uninitiated when it comes to knowing what goes on between men and women. I'd be very surprised if he and Sue have managed to hold out after nearly two years apart.'

'*You* would,' she said softly. 'Anyway, it's a different matter with them. They're in love.'

'While all we have is lust, I suppose. That didn't seem to bother you a few minutes ago.'

'Not surprisingly.' She moistened her lips with the tip of her tongue, caught his look and abruptly desisted. 'It makes me wonder just how many women you've made love to to have acquired that much expertise!'

'I don't keep a tally board, but thanks for the compliment.'

'It wasn't meant to be a compliment.'

'I know. That's another department where men and women differ. Talking of expertise, you're not without know-how yourself. Too many women think it's enough just to make themselves available without giving anything back. You've obviously learned better.'

She flushed. 'Ever heard of instinct?'

'Sure.' He took out cigarettes and lit one, eyed her for a moment through the smoke, then gave an impatient shake of his head. 'For God's sake why can't you come clean?'

'All right,' she said with deliberation, 'I've slept with dozens of men—so many I've lost count. Young ones, old ones, rich or poor, I didn't care! I'm a regular nymphomaniac! Is that what you wanted to know?'

His jawline tightened. 'You're asking for it!'

At that precise moment Jaime couldn't have cared less what she was asking for. 'I'd like to get changed,' she said wearily. 'Do you mind?'

The shrug came heavily. 'You'll tell me before we're through.'

'And then what?'

'And then maybe we can start fresh.'

'Mutual trust and understanding?' It was a calculated sneer. 'You couldn't sustain it even if I could. We're as incompatible as they come, Liam, and we both know it.'

'All right then, we'll have to settle for what we can get out of it.' He stubbed the cigarette viciously in the tray and started for the door. 'Tonight, tomorrow night and every other bloody night until we've both had enough!'

Jaime didn't bother going down to tea; it was more

than she could stomach. Dinner was another matter. She couldn't stay up here in her room for ever, Tris had to be faced some time. She put on the green velvet skirt she had worn that very first evening, along with a silky sweater because the air had turned chilly since teatime. Her eyes in the mirror looked bruised, with great dark circles underneath. She covered up the latter with an extra layer of make-up and briefly contemplated asking Tris to run her to the station in the morning—knowing full well she wouldn't. This was between her and Liam and no one else. She would have to handle it the best way she could.

CHAPTER TEN

JAIME hardly knew whether to be dismayed or relieved to find Tris on his own in the drawing room when she got down. Liam had gone down to the stables again, he told her, and wasn't back yet. He avoided looking at her directly as he added on a gruff note:

'Sorry about this afternoon. I thought you were asleep when you didn't answer.'

It would have been better for everyone, Jaime concluded, if he hadn't mentioned the episode at all. As he had she was bound to find some kind of reply. She forced a smile.

'Forget it, Tris.'

'I can't,' he said. 'I didn't think it was that kind of relationship. Not yet at any rate.'

Does your brother know any other? she was tempted to ask, but refrained. 'Jealous?' she asked instead. 'You'd rather think of me carrying a torch for you the rest of my days, I suppose?' She saw his expression change and made a contrite little gesture. 'Sorry, that was a rotten crack.'

'Yes, it was.' The pause stretched. 'You've changed,' he burst out at length. 'In just two weeks you've become another person, Jaime.'

'Oh, less than that. It's only just over a week ago since Liam asked me to go away with him.' Saying it like that brought the fact home with a sense of shock. *One* short week, not two. 'He isn't easy to say no to,' she added with truth.

'Does that mean you're going to marry him?'

She was saved from replying by the sound of a car pulling up on the drive out front.

'Susan,' said Tris, coming to his feet. 'I'd have put her off except that I thought you two had to get together some time. Stay where you are, I'll bring her in.'

'Try leaving us alone for a few minutes,' Jaime suggested. 'It might help break the ice.'

To do her credit, Susan seemed determined there should be none. She came in without hesitation, crossing directly to where Jaime stood to put a pair of warm lips briefly to her cheek.

'That,' she said, 'is for not making things difficult for Tris and me when you could so easily have done. With any luck, we might even become friends as well as sisters-in-law.' She sat down, tossing her purse carelessly into a corner of the settee. 'Tris went to phone the stud from the study.' Her smile was fleeting. 'No pun intended. How has Liam taken it?'

'Losing three foals?' Jaime shook her head. 'He hasn't said much about it.'

'Then it's hit him hard. He always clammed up over things that meant something to him. I remember when Lillian ...' She broke off, revealing the first sign of discomfiture. 'Sorry, she was the last person I meant to talk about. I suppose you did know about her?'

'Of course,' Jaime said steadily. 'She was the reason Liam took me with him to the States.'

'From what I remember of her, that must have been a real blow to her ego.'

'Enough to make her up and leave her husband while we were still there.'

'He's probably well rid.'

Recalling her last glimpse of Hal's aged-overnight

features, Jaime wondered about that. Someone could be hell to live with—but worse to live without.

'Jaime ...' Susan's voice was tentative ... 'would you think it too presumptuous of me if I said something?'

'About Liam and me?'

'Yes.'

Jaime's shrug held a lightness she was a long way from feeling. 'It's all been said. If you can't have one brother go for the other.'

'I don't think you're half the cynic you're trying to make out,' came the soft protest. 'You didn't get engaged to Liam just to get back at Tris. You must feel something for him.'

Jaime controlled a sudden impulsive longing to tell this other girl the whole sorry story. It would be such a relief to tell it to someone. She was glad when Tris chose that moment to come back into the room.

'Liam is on his way up,' he announced. 'Said he'd lost track of the time. The crisis seems over, by the way. Harstead thinks the rest will recover.'

His presence placed constriction on both girls. Jaime even found herself welcoming the sound of Liam's car. He put his head round the drawing room door in passing, flicking a smile in Susan's direction.

'Just give me ten minutes or so to wash and change, then I'll join you.'

He was down again in time for a quick drink before they ate, tall and vital in black slacks and a matching shirt with a dark red scarf tucked into the open neckline. He sat down beside Jaime on the settee close enough for her to feel the pressure of his thigh against hers when he leaned forward to put his glass on the table. He knew what his nearness did to her, of course; he couldn't fail to know. If he kept his promise to come to her room tonight she wouldn't be able to help herself. And he knew that too.

'I'm so glad you've managed to save the rest of the foals,' Susan said. 'Does the vet have any idea what the virus was yet?'

'No, the lab's still working on it, apparently. Seems to be an entirely new strain. What we have to try and isolate is the cause. It could have come in with the feed or the bedding, or even through one of the visiting mares.'

Jaime said, 'I thought it only attacked the young animals?'

'It has so far, but that doesn't mean an older one couldn't be a carrier. It attacks the respiratory system. Rather like pneumonia in a human: the lungs solidify.' His jaw set. 'It's a lousy way to die. Ted had to put the filly down this afternoon once it became obvious we weren't going to save it.'

What tenderness there was in him seemed reserved only for his horses, Jaime thought with a pang. Ridiculous to feel jealous of dumb animals, but she was and there was no denying it. Maybe he considered them the only creatures unlikely to let him down.

'You really think it's safe for Morning Star to come straight here tomorrow?' she asked.

'Ted seems to think so, although we'll be keeping her isolated for a few days anyway until she's over the journey.' He paused, added to the room in general,' I thought we might take a run out Castleton way after dinner. There's usually a dance on Friday nights.' His glance round at Jaime held a familiar glint. 'Not quite New York standards, but there'll be compensations.'

'I'm game,' said Susan. 'I haven't been to a Friday night special in ages. Be crowded, I suppose. They always were.'

That proved the understatement of the year. Crushed around a table at one end of the totally inadequate side room of a pub, they were too close to the four-man group to converse in any comfort, and hemmed in by the close-packed mass of gyrating humanity occupying the floor.

'City exodus,' Tristan had commented on arrival. 'You'd think it was the promised land!'

Jaime had a Pimms bristling with fruit until the glass was almost hidden. Lifting it with difficulty to her lips, she caught Liam's eye and had to smile.

'I've never tackled one of these things before,' she confessed, leaning towards him to make herself heard above the hubbub. 'Do you drink it or eat it?'

'Come and dance,' he said, ignoring the question.

Somehow he found a space large enough to take the two of them. Dancing in any way apart was difficult. Liam didn't even try. Held securely and a little too closely against the broad chest, Jaime registered her increased heartbeat and knew he must feel it too.

'Relax,' he said in her ear. 'You're stiff as a board. I'm hardly going to start anything here.'

'Why did you suggest coming?' she mouthed back in the same way because that was the only way they could communicate with any degree of success. 'This isn't your scene.'

'I thought it might be yours,' he said. 'Tris took you to discos in town, didn't he?'

'Places where you could breathe, not like this.'

'*This* is all there is—unless you go further afield to Manchester or Sheffield, and even then they're mostly for the teenagers. There's the Country Club, of course. I'm a member, but I don't think I've been in five years.'

'Why bother telling me?' she asked. 'I'm not going to be here very long.'

'We haven't decided on that yet. Depends how things go.' The movement of his hand on her hip was promise and threat together. 'I'm going to teach you to ride while you're here.'

'I don't want to learn!'

'You will once you're mounted.' He was mocking her, mouth derisive. 'It's another experience. Seven-thirty? Or maybe we'd better make it later, considering.'

'My room door is solid oak,' she reminded him caustically. 'I doubt if even you could get through that!'

'I can always relieve you of the key.'

'I thought you might do that, so I went through the spare rooms until I found another that fitted. It's well hidden.'

'Clever girl. Lock that door tonight and I'll have the lock off in the morning.'

'You wouldn't!'

'Try me.'

She was quiet for a moment, sensing the smouldering anger under the calm and wondering at the root cause.

'What about Tris?' she said at last. 'You wouldn't want him to know what's going on.'

'After catching us this afternoon *in flagrante delicto* he'd hardly be surprised.'

'He did not!' Her face was hot.

'Not far off it. Anyway, make no mistake, we're sharing a room tonight, tomorrow...'

'And every other bloody night,' she finished for him. 'I heard you the first time!'

His hands tightened. 'If there's one thing I hate it's hearing a woman swear!'

'Good. I'll make sure I do it more often.' She stopped, breathing hard, hating him, loving him, wanting him all at the same time. No matter how brutally he treated her, if didn't seem to make any difference in that respect. There had to be something wrong with her to still be here taking it from him.

'My rent on the flat is due in another week,' she said suddenly. 'I counted on having another job by now.'

'I'll take care of it.'

'I don't want you paying for it!'

'Can you?'

She could, but only just. She bit her lip. 'There are things I'm going to need anyway. I can't keep living out of one suitcase.'

'All right,' he said. 'I'll run you down next week to collect some.'

'Tris is hardly going to expect me to live at Oakleigh yet,' she protested. 'I could go back to town and let the whole thing peter out from there.'

'Except that I'm not ready to have it peter out—especially at a distance.' He drew her closer, running his lips down her hairline just above her ear. 'Judging from this afternoon's performance we're going to find total compatibility in one department at least. You're sensuous, Jaime. You hide it well under that cool, calm and collected pose, but it's there inside you just waiting to be let loose. I want to hold those beautiful breasts of yours in my hands again and make you quiver for more the way you did this afternoon. I want to undress you slowly—kiss every part of you—feel you under me.'

'Stop it!' she hissed. Her whole body felt on fire, her legs weak at the knees. 'Just stop it, Liam! You're not being fair!'

'I'm not trying to be fair. I'm making sure you forget about locking that door tonight.' His voice was low, but there was nothing soft about it. 'Hal couldn't have given you what you need from a man, any more than he could Lillian.'

'Bastard!' The word was torn from her. 'He's worth three of you!'

'Oh, quite a bit more than that. He's a millionaire several times over. And I said don't swear!'

'I want to go.' She tried to draw away from him but was held hard, the jut of his jaw a warning not to try insisting. Voice thick and unsteady, she muttered, 'God, I hate you! More than I thought it possible to hate anybody. You don't know the meaning of charity!'

'But I know how to make you say yes to me,' he taunted. 'And you'll say it again. It's going to be better than ever before, Jaime—for both of us. You'll tell me that too before we're through.'

'I'm not going to tell you anything,' she said through her teeth, 'because it isn't going to happen. I'm sick of being called a liar!'

'Then stop being one. That's all it takes.'

'For what?'

He looked down at her with sudden, unreadable change of expression. 'That rather depends.'

'On what my confession comes up with, I suppose.' Her tone bit, low as it was. 'How many other men could you accept as reasonable? Two? Four?'

'That isn't what I'm talking about.'

'Then what is?'

'A little word called honesty.'

'Oh, I see. Sinner, know thyself!' Her laugh sounded brittle. 'I wonder what kind of penance you'd consider fitted the bill? Hair shirts are right out of fashion.'

'I'll give it some thought.' His eyes dropped to her mouth, registering the faint quiver of her lower lip with cynical expression. 'You know, you missed your real vocation. You could act Bernhardt into a cocked hat! If I didn't keep being presented with evidence to the contrary I'd believe every damned word you said.' He stopped moving to the music and let her go, turning her in front of him to direct her off the floor. 'Let's find the others and get out of here.'

The drive back to Oakleigh was accomplished in near silence, nobody apparently disposed towards light conversation. Susan declined to come indoors when they reached the house, preferring, she said, to drive straight on home. Tris accompanied her across to her own car, leaving Jaime and Liam to make their way inside.

'Coffee?' he asked when they reached the hall. 'Pax will still be up.'

She shook her head, not looking at him. 'I'm going to bed.'

'I know,' he said. He reached out before she was aware of his intention and turned her towards him, held her there for a moment studying her face, then bent to find her mouth with his in a kiss that set every nerve end jangling. 'That's just for starters,' he said when he finally put her from him. He ran a light finger down the long line of her throat, smiling at her involuntary tremor. 'I don't somehow think you'll be turning that key.'

Jaime didn't answer. She was incapable of it. She went up the stairs without glancing back, reaching her room and shutting the door to lean her weight against it with closed eyes. The imprint of Liam's mouth still lingered along with the line he had traced over her skin. She wanted him with everything in her.

It took every ounce of self-persuasion she could bring to bear to reach a hand behind her and slowly turn the key in the lock. Under other circumstances the choice would have been clear-cut and inevitable, but not for anything was she going to make love with a man who believed her a liar and a tramp. Let him suffer the humiliation of being rejected. She could at least gain some small consolation in that.

She was sitting fully clothed still on the end of the bed when he came along to her door. Frozenly she watched the knob turn and stop, and waited with bated breath for the sound of his voice.

For a few seconds all was still and quiet, then the knob was released and she heard him moving away down the corridor again, his tread neither quicker nor slower than it had been coming. She had to forcibly restrain herself from jumping to her feet and tearing open the door to call him back.

She got down at eight on the Saturday morning, asked a poker-faced Mrs Paxton for toast and coffee and wondered what was going on behind the dour expression. The woman had disliked her from the first, and this latest development was hardly scheduled to change her mind. She probably considered Liam deprived of all his senses to have done what he apparently had.

The latter came into the dining room while she was still there. He was wearing riding breeches and boots along with a chequered shirt. He poured himself coffee from the pot without speaking, then swung a chair round to straddle it comfortably where he could look across at Jaime's averted face.

'I spent quite a few hours last night considering the alternatives,' he said almost conversationally. 'There seem to be three. I can send you back to where you came from and write you off; I can take you by force as you're asking for, but which doesn't happen to appeal much to me ...' he paused for a brief moment before going on ... 'or I can marry you like you're angling for and have the double satisfaction.'

Her head came up at that point. 'Double?'

'There's more than one way of putting a woman like you down. You'd toe the line as my wife—in every respect.' His mouth was sardonic. 'Think it might be worth it?'

'For someone supposedly holding out for marriage I almost lost out yesterday, didn't I?' she said, ignoring the question. 'If Tris hadn't...'

'You knew he'd be coming. He said he told you he'd call you for tea. You're the cleverest little schemer I know, but still a schemer.' There was something in the grey eyes she couldn't fathom. 'Right from the first minute you realised I was lusting after you, that mind of yours started ticking over. Tris, after all, wouldn't have come into any of this unless I died without heirs.'

'You persuaded me to go to the States with you,' Jaime protested.

'You didn't take much persuading. You were caught between two fires when Lillian left the field open the way she did—except that divorces don't always come off, and you didn't want to be left with jam on your face. That fairy story you told Tris was a brilliant move. To be let down by one Caine was bad enough in his estimation, but *two*! I'd have forfeited every ounce of his respect and regard if I'd tried to explain the position. He isn't ready to hear a word against the girl who let him go as easily and uncomplainingly as you did.'

She stared at him numbly for a long moment, trying to find some hole in his reasoning, no matter how minute. It was like a conspiracy, she thought: the whole weight of evidence piled up gainst her just as if it really had been planned from the start. And Liam. What kind of man was it who could offer marriage to someone he regarded with such contempt? Sitting here looking at him now it was difficult to read anything but strength of character into those hard-hewn features, yet what he contemplated revealed little of that quality. Wanting her was no excuse.

Ego-swelling, she supposed cynically, when it came with such intensity, but still no excuse.

'There seems to be just one small thing you've overlooked,' she said at last with a calm that surprised herself. 'To confirm everything you've just laid out I have to say yes to marrying you.'

His face gave nothing away. 'And?'

'And the answer is no.'

'Pride?' he asked. 'It's a bit late for that.' He put down his cup and hoisted himself to his feet. 'You'll change your mind—after a proper interval to try and change mine. It's the best offer you're ever likely to get, and you know it.'

'Why?' she whispered. 'Taking everything you've said as the truth, why are you giving in like this?'

He studied her before replying, eyes moving over the face framed by the heavy, coppery fall of her hair, then down over that part of her not hidden by the table, lingering on the slipped top button of her shirt. 'Because you're driving me up the wall,' he said levelly. 'I want you, but I want you willingly, and if marriage is what it takes to make you willing then you've got it. What we do with it is something else. Maybe I can succeed with you where I failed with Lillian. There's one thing for sure, you won't be doing to me what she did to Hal!'

'I won't have the chance,' she said, 'because I won't marry you.' Her fingers were clenched around her cup, seeking warmth from the liquid within. 'I mean it, Liam. I *won't* marry you!'

'Methinks the lady doth protest too much.' He put a hand on her nape and took hold of a handful of hair, drawing back her head to his bruising kiss, making her respond to him by sheer force of will. His eyes were glittering when he lifted his mouth from hers again.

'That's one thing we do have in common—a matching libido. Pull yourself together and come on down to the stables. I'm putting you up on your first horse.'

'Liam, please can't we talk this whole thing over?' Her voice was low and scratchy. 'I can't...'

'That's what we've just done. Subject closed.' He wound a single tendril of her hair about a finger, then let it go, watching it corkscrew with a faint twist of his lips. 'Don't start getting cold feet now. Marriage to me might not be quite the bed of roses you maybe envisaged at first, but I can promise you it won't be dull. We'll go up to town and do it quietly without telling anybody. That way we don't steal any thunder from the wedding Sue and Tris are planning for next month. No need to keep on the flat beyond the end of the month now. You'll have a whole house to help run.' His tone hardened. 'No doubt you'll cope.'

Jaime went through the rest of the day like an automaton, barely registering the things she did. The riding lesson was probably a greater success for her lack of will-power. She just let her hands and feet obey Liam's instructions and the horse itself did the rest. Afterwards she couldn't even have said whether she had been riding a bay or a chestnut, it had meant that little.

'You'll soon pick it up,' Liam told her when he eventually let her get down. 'I'll have you galloping inside a couple of weeks. You'll fall off, of course, that's inevitable. It takes at least seven falls to make a rider. Think you can stand it?'

She turned her back on him, unable to bear the innuendo any longer. Was this what life would be like if they went through with what he had planned? she wondered dully. *If?* Was there any doubt? She didn't seem to have any volition of her own left in her. What Liam was offering hardly constituted a good basis to build on, but at least it would keep her with him, give her the chance to make him see how wrong he had been all along about her. And if she never quite managed that, he might be persuaded to put it aside—might even gain satisfaction from believing he had succeeded in making a one-man woman of the supposed little tramp.

Excuses, she told herself in wry disgust, but it didn't help. She was going to do what Liam wanted because she didn't have the strength of mind to turn him down.

CHAPTER ELEVEN

THEY drove down to London on the Monday morning after a weekend Jaime for one felt she would not have liked to live through again.

There had been no question of deciding how she spent her nights because Liam hadn't attempted to come near her. We'll save it, he'd said with self-directed mockery. A wedding night to remember. Isn't that what every bride really wants?

The flat was just as she had left it a bare week ago. So much had happened since she could scarcely believe it was so short a time. They had eaten on the way. Liam saw her in but declined to stay for the coffee she offered to prepare, saying there were arrangements to make.

Alone at last, Jaime sat for a long time in the little sitting room trying to sort herself out. At the end of an hour she was no closer. All she did know was that her own motives bore no more credit than Liam's. What they felt for one another was no basis for marriage. One solution, she supposed cynically, was to become his mistress instead of his wife and retain at least some of her self-respect. Except that they could hardly carry on that kind of relationship at Oakleigh, and she couldn't see Liam willing to make the journey down here to London on a regular basis.

No, the die was cast. She either married him or lost him—and that latter she couldn't bring herself to do. She should think herself darn lucky that he himself had considered force an inadequate satisfaction, because most men wouldn't have seen it that way under the circumstances. Not that he would have had to use much had he only realised it, she acknowledged wryly. She would have been melting into his arms within minutes of his making the first move—no matter what the circumstances.

She made herself some coffee and a sandwich when he still hadn't returned at six, and barely touched either. Supposing he had changed his mind? she thought. The hold she had over him was purely physical, after all. Perhaps he had come to his senses and realised just what that was really worth long-term.

Wandering around the flat, she found herself viewing her reflection in the bedroom mirror with assessing eyes, trying to work out what she had that could make a man like Liam consider marrying her just to possess. Her features were good but not outstanding, her chief claim to beauty lying in the thick mane of copper hair framing them. Her figure ... well, she had drawn enough wolf whistles in her time to know it followed the lines men seemed to like, yet so did those of thousands of other girls. There was nothing unique about her; no special quality which set her aside. The only thing she could come up with was what Liam had said the other morning when he'd told her what they were going to do: a matching libido. Was that so important to a man that he'd contemplate sacrificing everything because of it?

The ring of the doorbell at seven brought a sensation closely akin to drowning. If this wasn't him now he wouldn't be coming. She was suddenly certain of that.

He had changed into a pale grey three-piece suit worn with a dark grey shirt and a silver-coloured tie—that was the first thing she noted about him when she opened the door. He watched her observing him with sardonic expression, one hand against the jamb.

'Do I get to come in or do I stand out here while *you* change?' he asked.

She stood back without a word, closing the door behind him and turning to stand with her back to him in a position almost defensive.

'Change for what?'

'I've tickets for a theatre, followed by dinner and late cabaret!' His mouth twisted afresh. 'Call it a celebration. We get married Wednesday at two-thirty—civil ceremony, of course. That should give you plenty of time to get things together. You won't be slipping up to town every five minutes once we get back to Oakleigh.'

'I wouldn't expect to.' Jaime went quiet for a moment, barely knowing what else to say. 'Special licence?' was all she could find.

'Common.' He seemed to take pleasure in emphasising the word. 'The other is a dispensation only granted in cases of emergency, and I doubt if the Archbishop would consider ours as such.' He glanced at his watch. 'You've got fifteen minutes if you want to make the first act.'

'Where ...' she began.

'The Garrick. Sorry if you'd have preferred a musical.' He didn't sound it.

'I don't much like musicals,' she said truthfully, and hesitated. 'Liam, I ...'

'Go and get ready.' He moved away and sat down, taking up a magazine from the rack in a manner which left her little choice but to obey.

She wore a simple, long-sleeved dress in plain navy blue which fastened all the way down the front with tiny buttons from a modest V neckline and sat smoothly over her hips, teaming it with a cameo pinned to a narrow velvet ribbon about her neck. She felt neither happy nor unhappy, just in limbo.

'I gather you've booked yourself into a hotel,' she said when she went back.

'Browns,' he said. 'Cuts the temptation. I'll put you in a taxi when the time comes. This way you don't have to worry about holding out till Wednesday night.'

'Is it going to be like this the whole time?' she asked, biting her lip. 'Because I don't think I can go through with it if it is.' She made herself go on, despite the irony in his expression. 'You might not believe it, but I'm marrying you because I love you, Liam. I don't know why, you've given me little enough cause. But women are like that—we go against reason. If I had any real sense I'd tell you to get out of here right now.'

'Yes,' he said, 'you would.' He put out a commanding hand. 'Come here.'

Jaime went despite herself, wishing she had the guts to do as she had just said. He didn't believe her; that was apparent from his manner now. He thought it just part of the act.

The kiss was scorching and it went on for ever. All it lacked was any element of feeling beyond physical hunger.

'*That*,' he said, when he finally put her away from him, 'is what I can make you feel for me, so don't let's try dressing it up with fancy names to salve any last-minute flutters of conscience. You're about as capable of love as any calculating machine!'

'Machines don't have a conscience,' she pointed out on a husky note, knowing it was useless. 'Not even a flicker. And it's hardly the last minute yet either.'

The grey eyes mocked. 'So it isn't. I'll have to tread carefully for the next couple of days, won't I?'

Jaime had no idea what the play they saw was about. For two hours they watched various characters moving about the single set, listened to them speaking their lines, laughed dutifully on occasion when everyone else in the audience signified a humorous moment and couldn't even have told anyone the title afterwards, much less who had been playing whom, well known as the names were.

They had a drink at the bar during the interval, thoughtfully ordered by Liam before the curtain went up. Watching him carrying them across to the table they had managed to secure, Jaime thought how insignificant he made other men in the place look. It was difficult to believe that by this time on Wednesday they would be man and wife. Could she really go through with it, no matter how she felt about him? If it came to that, could she even get through the coming long hours between?

The dinner and cabaret he had promised turned out to be in a classy but unmistakable revue bar. She knew he had chosen the place purposely, but refrained from complaint, determined to accept everything she saw without blinking an eyelid.

Liam ordered champagne to go with the meal, refilling her glass every time she got halfway down it. At her invitation, he had chosen the food himself: egg stuffed with soft caviar and served in a bed of spring salmon, followed by fillets of beef cooked in herbs with gypsy sauce and tender asparagus tips. There were few other women in the place, Jaime noted. Perhaps half a dozen, apart from the hostesses.

The latter were not what she would have anticipated, the dresses they wore neither too revealing nor flashy in design. Sensing her regard, one of them seated at a nearby table with a couple of business types out on the town gave her a friendly smile. Jaime smiled back, caught Liam's mockingly lifted brow and refused to drop her eyes from his.

'Another first,' she said. 'You really do know all the best places!'

The revue began while they were still only halfway through eating, and once again she found any preconceived ideas going by the board. Far from being the rather sleazy, risqué performance suggested by the name of the place, it turned out to be extremely well staged, with a chorus line which could have come straight from the Folies Bergère. There were strippers, of course, but only the young and the lovely, offensive only to those who saw exploitation in what they were doing. Jaime wasn't sure how she regarded it in that sense herself. Revealing oneself in public for money could hardly be called a creditable occupation, yet to these girls it was obviously a job they enjoyed. In the end she came to the conclusion that she wouldn't do it herself and left it at that.

At intervals throughout the revue she sensed Liam's eyes on her face judging her reactions, and was hard put not to glance his way or show some other response. Only when the last ostrich feather had whisked away and the music started for dancing again did she allow herself to look at him, smiling a smile she hoped appeared natural.

'What comes next, a boat ride on the river?'

His shrug was light. 'If that's what you'd like. Do you want some fresh coffee?'

'No,' she said, 'but I would like to dance.'

He got up without protest, and pulled back her chair, leading her out between the two tables in front on to the floor. She longed to melt against him; to slide her arms up and about his neck and feel him hold her close, but without his encouragement she couldn't bring herself to make the move.

He held her lightly several inches away from him, jaw

on a level with her eyes. His hands were warm and dry, strength tempered in the lean fingers. A smile touched the corners of his lips as he looked down at her. Following the line of his glance, Jaime saw that the top button of her dress had come open and made a movement to fasten it again, only to have him hold her hand fast.

'In theatre language, the line across the proscenium arch is called the tormentor,' he observed on a dry note. 'Leave it the way it is. Torment is supposed to be good for the soul.'

'Liam, don't,' she said low-toned. 'Please can't we find some way to be together without this sort of thing? If you detest me so much why are you marrying me at all?'

'You know why.' His smile was mirthless. 'I'm going to enjoy turning you into a wife to be proud of. You're the one who should be doing the running—but you're not, are you.'

'No,' she said. 'I must have a death wish!'

'I don't intend killing you.'

'Not with kindness, at any rate. I don't imagine you'd know how to start being kind!'

'I told you once, I treat as I find. Try being a little more submissive and I might be persuaded to cut out the aggression. It's in your hands.'

She looked back at him unflinchingly. 'No, it isn't, it's in *your* mind. It always has been.'

'We'll see.' He studied her a moment, then seemed suddenly to relent, features relaxing a little. 'You're probably right. We make our own bed and lie on it. All right, let's make out there's no past for the present and enjoy what we've got.' He pulled her closer, sliding both hands around her back and putting his lips to her temple. 'One more night,' he said softly, 'and then I'm going to own you—body and soul. Can you take it, Jaime? Being owned, I mean. Will the return be worth the sacrifice?'

'If I didn't think so I wouldn't be making it,' she said, and he laughed.

'I'll remind you of that.'

They danced in silence after that for a while. Held the way Liam was holding her now, Jaime could almost forget the way things really were and lose herself in dreams of how they could be. To have Liam in love with her would be heaven—even to have him believe her would be a start in the right direction. She placed no reliance on proving herself on Wednesday night. Hadn't she warned him it was possible to act that part? He wouldn't have forgotten those ill-chosen words.

'You'd better buy some proper riding togs while you're in town,' he said out of the blue, startling her and maddening her at one and the same time. 'A well-fitting hat is essential.'

'Can't you think of anything else but horses?' she queried frigidly, and saw his mouth straighten.

'That's something else you're going to have to learn to accept. The stud is my life—has been ever since I was forced to come home and settle down when my father died.'

'I suppose you preferred jet-setting!'

'I was no more a jet-setter than you are now,' he came back impatiently. 'I had a job that entailed a lot of travelling, that's all. If Tris had been in a position to take over the estate for me he could have had the lot.'

'But not now.'

'Naturally not now. He's the unfortunate brother, only succeeding if I produce no heirs.'

Jaime shied hastily away from the obvious connotations. 'What will you do when they're married? Divide the house into two wings?'

'They won't be living at Oakleigh. Tris wouldn't want it any more than I would. They're buying a house on the other side of Bakewell.' His hands had hardened a fraction, his mouth tilting. 'So you see, it will be just the two of us after next month.'

'Apart from Mrs Paxton.'

'She won't interfere.' His gaze mocked her. 'Scared?'

She shook her head, refusing to let him get to her. 'Providing I keep my side of the bargain I doubt if I'll need to be.'

'And what do you see as your side of the bargain?'

'You said it yourself—submission: doing as I'm told, keeping a low profile; thinking twice before I smile at another man.'

He was looking at her with narrowed eyes as if trying to penetrate through to the mind behind her own. 'How long do you think that will last?'

'I haven't the slightest idea. Till I get sickened of trying to convince you, I suppose.'

'Or bored.' The pause was brief. 'There's one way of taking care of that. With a baby you wouldn't have time to be bored.'

Something contracted sharply in Jaime's chest. A baby —Liam's son; dark like his father, and dependent on her the way Liam would never be. Or perhaps a girl, a pretty, dainty little daughter who would soften that heart of his. She said with bitterness, 'Are you sure I'd make a fitting mother for your children?'

'You'd have to.' He gaven a sudden sigh, expression undergoing a subtle change. 'Oh, God, what's the use! Jaime, I ...'

Someone bumped into them from behind, the man looking round to apologise. Jaime felt her heart lurch sickeningly as she met the startled eyes. Oh no, not now! How cruel could fate be?

'Well, who would have expected to see you here!' said Gerald. 'Must be—what—all of two years?' From the tone of his voice he recalled the details of their parting with clarity. His glance towards Liam was speculative. 'How are things going these days?'

'I'm fine.' There was nothing for it; she was going to have to introduce them. She didn't dare look at Liam as she did so, aware of his reaction to the name through the painful tension of his grasp. Not that he probably hadn't already recognised the other man.

'Fiancé, eh?' Gerald exclaimed with an odd inflection. For the first time he seemed to remember his own partner, glancing her way and sheering off again in a manner only too familiar to Jaime's memory. 'Janice Hunt,' he murmured. 'Jaime's a former secretary of mine, Janice.'

The woman smiled, her manner easy. She was in her late twenties, Jaime guessed, smooth, sophisticated and beautifully groomed, yet with warmth in her eyes. Not Gerald's type at all. She wondered what they were doing together.

'I'm one of your successors,' Janice was saying now. 'Comparatively new. I only started working for him a couple of weeks ago. It must be about two years since that office of his was properly organised. Did he throw files all over the place then too?' She didn't wait for an answer, her glance going to Liam who still hadn't spoken. 'Are you getting married soon?'

'Day after tomorrow,' he said. 'How about joining us in a glass of champagne?'

'Great idea,' Gerald chimed in. 'A toast to the bride and groom! Lead the way.'

Liam kept a hand on Jaime's shoulder as they went back to their table with the other two in tow. It hurt. Two more chairs were swiftly procured by one of the waiters, and the second bottle of Bollinger opened with a flourish and a festive pop.

'Much happiness,' said Janice, lifting her glass. Her

tone sounded genuine. 'Will you be living here in London?'

'Derbyshire,' Liam corrected. 'Near Bakewell.'

A look of sudden recognition sprang in her eyes. 'Are you the Caine behind the Oakleigh stud, by any chance?'

'That's right.' He was surprised and showed it. 'You're interested in horses?'

'Not me particularly, my brother. He's one of the show-jumping crowd. He bought a colt from you about three years ago—Silver Mount.'

'Of course. Gavin Hunt!' Liam was smiling himself now, with more warmth than Jaime had ever seen in him. 'They make a pretty good team.'

'Don't they! If he has as good a year this as last, he could finish up being short-listed for the Olympic team. He's always talking about coming back to Oakleigh for another look round. Do you have anything at present which might interest him?'

Liam laughed. 'Tell him three years from now I might have the ideal.'

'How's that?'

'I'm mating my stallion Oberon with a filly I just bought from Hal Lessing in the States. Gavin will know the potential.'

'I'll make sure to warn him.'

Gerald had leaned closer to Jaime, his after-shave too overwhelmingly memory provoking. Odd, she thought, how faithful men could be when it came to things like toiletries. They found an aroma they liked, and stuck to it through thick and thin.

'You've done well for yourself,' he murmured. 'Good luck.'

She looked at him to see if he meant it, and saw that he did. Something had mellowed him. Time—or Janice?

'Thanks,' she said. 'How are you, Gerald?'

'Oh, prospering. Business couldn't be better.' The fine head turned a little towards his companion, coming back with an ironical look about the eyes. 'It gets harder to keep up these days. Too many bright young men climbing the ladder.'

She would have liked to ask him what had happened to the girl she had seen him with less than a month ago, but of course one couldn't.

Conversation became general for a while, although neither man fully relaxed. When Jaime excused herself to visit the cloakroom, to her dismay Janice came too, leaving their respective partners together.

'They'll survive,' the other said, sensing her attitude. She leaned forward towards the mirror to touch up her lips, blotted them on a tissue from the box provided and gave Jaime an oblique glance. 'That's a fab man you've got there. Do you love him?'

The question should have taken her aback, yet oddly it didn't. 'Yes,' she said simply.

'Lucky girl.' There was no envy in her tone, just a certain wistfulness. 'That's the way to do it!'

Jaime found herself asking the question before she could stop herself. 'Are you and Gerald ...' She broke off in quick embarrassment. 'Sorry, I didn't mean ...'

'It's all right,' Janice answered with a faint smile. 'And yes, we are. It happened less than a week ago, and I was in full possession of all my faculties.' The smile widened a little at Jaime's expression. 'It wasn't the way I'd have chosen myself, but what about falling in love is sensible? I know what he is, and what he's been. I know he narrowly avoided being maimed for life by his latest secretary's boy-friend.' She paused before adding without change of tone, 'And I know about you, Jaime. No, don't look like that. What he told me about you was all to your credit. You pulled him up short, made him take a good clear look at himself for the first time in years. He's never forgotten it.'

Jaime sat down in the nearest chair, legs suddenly weak. 'It doesn't seem to have left any real impression,' she said. 'I saw him only weeks ago with the girl you've just spoken about—at least, I assume it must have been her. He was leading her on in exactly the same old way.'

'Ah, but that's Gerald, isn't it? And probably always will be. He's scared of getting old; constantly trying to prove to himself he can still make it with the younger generation if he wants to. But he says there's been nothing serious since you walked out on him.'

'He wasn't serious about me.'

'He was, you know. As far as he could be with a wife in the background. Why didn't he divorce her?' She shrugged lightly. 'For the same reason he won't be doing for me either: because he doesn't have the courage to make that final break. Guess I'm stuck with what I've got of him now.'

Jaime wondered for a wild moment if she could somehow get Janice to tell Liam what she had just told her, and knew even as she thought it that it was impossible. Liam would only think they had concocted the whole thing between them. His kind of doubt needed a steam-roller to squash it.

'You've understood him better in two weeks than I did in as many months,' she said softly.

'Yes, well, I had a father a bit like Gerald. My mother didn't understand *him* either while he was alive. It isn't always such a line.' Janice finished retouching her face and stood back, smoothing down her skirt. 'Shall we get back?'

The two men were sitting without talking when they reached the table. Janice made no move to sit down again, saying they should be going. Under her jurisdiction, leavetaking was accomplished easily and swiftly. Liam watched them move away, face enigmatic.

'Fine woman,' he said.

'Yes.' Jaime couldn't resist it. '*She'd* have made you the perfect wife. She even knows something about horses.'

'So will you,' he said obliquely, 'given the right kind of instruction. Do you want to dance again, or would you rather leave?'

'You mean you don't want to watch another performance?'

'The second show isn't until one-thirty. I'm not putting you in a taxi at three o'clock in the morning, and I'm sure you wouldn't want me driving you back myself.'

He was the only one who was so sure. Jaime almost wished he would—get it over.

'You're right,' she said. 'According to your lights, I've too much to lose. We'll go now.'

There was a taxi just depositing a party when they got outside, obviously candidates for the second performance. Liam grabbed it for her, putting her into the back and giving the driver the address.

'I'll meet you for lunch at the Ritz,' he said. 'One o'clock sharp. Any shopping you haven't got through by then we'll finish in the afternoon. Leave the riding gear till then anyway. I'll take you to the proper place.' He laid a hard kiss on her mouth and straightened, closing the door between them.

He was still standing where she had left him when the taxi returned down the far side of the road after making the intersection.

CHAPTER TWELVE

JAIME was in town for nine-thirty next morning, her shopping list short but essential. She chose her dress for the register office at Harrods, paying an exorbitant price for the simplicity of hand-stitched linen. She couldn't call it a wedding dress, but it was at least white. Let Liam curl his lip at the imagined irony as much as he liked!

With it she teamed shoes in navy and white, with a handbag to match and a floppy-brimmed hat in plain navy silk trimmed with a single, self-coloured band of pleated petersham. That, apart from minor items, was that. She refused to even glance in the direction of the lingerie department with all its floating, gossamer gowns suggestive of honeymoons. So far as she knew, they would be spending their wedding night right here in the capital before returning home to Oakleigh the following day.

Home. It sounded strange. It would be a long time before she could be able to look on it as really that.

Liam was waiting for her in the hotel foyer when she arrived at five minutes to the hour. She left her packages in the cloakroom with the attendant, checking her appearance in the neat brown shirtwaister before going to join him. Her skin had a glow about it that owed little to make-up. Twenty-five and a half hours to go. She was, she decided with a firmness born of near-desperation, going to let nothing spoil tomorrow. After that was something else again.

Conversation was limited, she found, by the number

of staff swarming in the restaurant. There seemed to be about four to each table, the coming and goings scheduled to make any sort of intimate tête-à-tête a practical impossibility. She wondered if Liam had chosen the place for that very reason.

'How did it feel?' he asked over coffee when they were at last left alone for a few minutes. He lifted a satirical eyebrow at her look of puzzlement. 'Last night, seeing your first love again. Or had all feeling died like it did over Tristan?'

'As a doornail.' Irrelevantly she thought how good he looked in the shadow-striped dark suit, shoulders wider by far than the curved back of the chair in which he sat. A conservative dresser, she supposed some might call him, but his style suited both his frame and his manner. Emotion, sudden and ungovernable, husked her throat. 'You were going to say something just before Gerald bumped into us last night,' she got out.

A shutter came down over the grey eyes. 'Was I?'

She ignored the flatness in his voice, chasing a crumb around the edge of her cheese plate with one prong of a clean fork. 'You said it was no use. *What* was no use, Liam? Were you going to tell me you'd changed your mind about marrying me?' Her head lifted then, her expression serious. 'It isn't too late.'

'I'm not changing my mind,' he said. 'And neither are you. Finish your coffee and we'll get off to Giddens. They'll kit you out with everything necessary.'

For a moment Jaime contemplated telling him she had no interest in learning to ride whatsoever, but it would have been both childish and untrue. She wanted to become part of his life, not stand aside from it.

Viewing herself an hour or so later in the long mirror, she had to admit that riding gear added a certain dash to one's appearance. The fawn jodhpurs fitted perfectly about waist and hips, disappearing into polished brown boots in supple calf. Her hacking jacket was brown too, in a tiny herringbone tweed. Later, Liam had said, when she was proficient enough, there would be another outfit in hunting black for riding to hounds. Jaime couldn't ever see herself getting that far, but she had refrained from saying so. Jump your fences when you come to them, she told herself dryly.

He nodded approval when she stepped out of the dressing room for his inspection, settling the hard hat a little more forward on her head.

'Like that,' he said. 'It isn't meant for decoration.' He looked at the hovering assistant. 'We'll take them with us.'

Outside again, he glanced up at the sky. 'Looks like rain. Anything else you need, or can we call it a day?'

She agreed at once, half hoping he would call it an evening too. The thought of another spent the way they had spent the last one was more than she could bear right now.

'I thought you might appreciate your last night of freedom on your own,' he said in the car, echoing her own idea. 'Time to clear up any loose ends at the flat and finish your packing. I'll pick you up for lunch about twelve.'

'Would you make it after lunch?' Jaime suggested in a small tight voice. 'I don't think I'll feel like eating a big meal.'

'All right then, after lunch. Say one-thirty.' He sounded unmoved. 'Have everything ready that you're taking with you. There's no going back.'

The hours stretched endlessly after he had gone, making her half wish she had asked him to stay. They might spar all the time they were together, but even that was preferable to this tearing emptiness.

She went to bed early, and lay awake for a long time looking out at the familiar corner of night sky through the bedroom window, wondering which quarter of it she would be viewing the following night. Liam had made no offer to tell her where they would be staying and she hadn't been able to bring herself to ask. She still took it for granted that they would be going straight to Oakleigh the day after. Honeymoons were for lovers in the finer sense. Their present relationship hardly qualified them as such.

There was still time to back out, she reminded herself, and knew she was grasping at straws. It had been too late the moment she had said yes to his proposal. In actual fact, she had never said the word in itself, she recalled, but the acceptance had been in her failure to say no, and mean it.

She'd work at this marriage, she promised herself fiercely. If it took her years she would make Liam love her in the end! She fell asleep clutching a mental image of the dark, arrogant man who would be her husband in every sense of the word by this time next day.

The morning was fine and warm and sunny. Liam arrived on the dot, his suit an unconservative pale blue which enhanced the tan he had deepened at Oakleigh over the weekend.

Jaime was ready except for her outer clothes. She opened the door to him wearing a flower-sprigged cotton housecoat she could push into her luggage at the last moment.

'Everything is ready,' she said, feeling more than a little tongue-tied with nerves now that the time was here.

'Just the suitcases and that bag there. I'm leaving the rest for the next tenant.'

He made no comment on that. There was none to make. Where she was going she certainly was not going to need kitchen utensils and such.

'I'll get this lot downstairs and wait for you in the car,' he said. 'There's plenty of time, so don't rush.'

The white dress seemed to steal all the colour from her cheeks when she had it on. She applied blusher high on her cheekbones, seeing the reflected sparkle in her eyes with a sense of fraud. The brim of the navy hat afforded a kind of protection, and she pulled it well down about her face.

Handing over the keys of the locked flat to the caretaker downstairs proved the worst moment. Now there really was no going back. The woman wished her luck, with a certain speculation in the swift glance she cast over her. Probably wondering if she were pregnant, Jaime reflected dryly, considering the suddenness with which things had been arranged.

Liam watched her coming from the driving seat of the Mercedes, getting out when she was a few feet away to come round and open the nearside door, eyes veiled. They were moving away from the kerb when he tossed the small package into her lap.

'Wedding present,' he said briefly. 'I noticed your old one was on its last legs.'

Jaime extracted the heavy gold bracelet watch with fingers gone numb, sliding it on to her wrist. 'It's beautiful,' she managed. 'Thank you, Liam.' It sounded totally inadequate, but what else was there to say?

Half an hour later it was all over. Emerging from the comparative gloom of the register office into bright sunshine again, Jaime wondered why she felt no different.

Apart from the gold band on her finger there was nothing to tell her she was now Mrs Caine. Liam had their marriage certificate firmly tucked away. She supposed he would show it to her if she asked, but saw no way of doing so which wouldn't sound totally odd.

'Hungry?' he queried when they were back in the car again. 'Or would you rather wait for dinner when we arrive?'

'Yes,' she said, and glanced at him questioningly. 'Arrive where?'

'We're going north. Back to Derbyshire.' There was a note in his voice she couldn't quite fathom. 'Where else?'

Where else indeed? Oakleigh awaited them. Home now for them both. Yet surely it would have been better to have left it until tomorrow to make their return? Liam must have warned them they were coming. They would more than likely all be waiting—Tris and Susan, Libby and Michael—champagne at the ready to greet the errant bride and groom. How was she going to bear that hollow mockery?

Too late for regrets, she reminded herself, stiffening her backbone. She had wanted Liam and now she had got him—for better or worse. If the latter came first then she would simply have to live through it.

Traffic was heavy, and it took them an age to reach the outskirts and the run-on to the motorway. Liam made no attempt to push the speed even then, settling down to a steady seventy which barely necessitated any overtaking. Jaime liked the way he handled a car, relaxed but in control, hands strong and brown on the wheel. Tonight he would control her in just the same way, making her respond to his every touch. Was that why men called their cars 'she'—because they got the same kind of feeling of possession?

They left the motorway just after six at an exit way down from the one Tris had taken that first time. Jaime said nothing, assuming Liam had decided on another route home, and not at all loath to leave the sheer tedium of motorway driving.

The nights were drawing out, the light still full and golden. There could be nowhere lovelier than the English countryside in weather like this, she thought, viewing the green slopes of hill and dale, the fresh canopy of the trees. There were wild flowers in the hedgerows, the colours singing and alive the way they could never be within the confines of a city with all its attendant dirt and fumes. This part of her new life at least she was going to enjoy without restriction.

It was only on entering the small market town that it finally came home to her just where Liam was headed. Heart jerking, she watched the all too familiar square pass by the window, waiting for the left-hand turn beyond which would prove her right.

He took it without hesitation, heading out along the road that led past the Huntingtower Hotel to turn into the car park some moments later and bring the Mercedes to a standstill. Jaime slowly turned her head to meet the cynical grey eyes, her breath drawn in with difficulty pas the obstruction in her throat.

'You swine,' she said.

'Third time.' The words were measured. 'We saw each other for the very first time right here. It seemed an appropriate spot to start another phase. Which case do you want taking in?'

'None. I'm not going in there with you.'

'You are, if I have to carry you. I suppose one threshold is as good as another.' He came round and opened her door, standing there waiting with a line to his mouth she knew was not going to relent. 'We're booked here for the next two nights. I've business in town to take care of before we go back to Oakleigh.'

'Killing two birds with one stone?' she flashed, and saw a flicker of a smile cross his lips.

'One of them just gets her wings clipped, that's all. Now come on out.'

She obeyed because there wasn't a great deal else she could do but invite humiliation by being forced to accompany him. Liam went to get the necessary luggage from the boot, then led the way inside.

It was just as she remembered it, the reception desk set at the rear of the beamed lobby under the curve of the old staircase. Jaime didn't recall the man who checked them in, although that was hardly surprising. Her mind had been on other matters that night two years ago. Regardless of everything, she could only be thankful that Liam stood here with her now instead of Gerald. She might be a fool for loving a man who could hurt her this way, but she did. She even understood him—so far as this went, at any rate.

Their room was on the same landing; she was surprised he hadn't gone all the way and booked the same number. But perhaps his memory had let him down there. There were two large windows, a double divan bed covered by a beautifully worked patchwork quilt, fitted carpets on the floor and a washhand basin set into a mirrored alcove on the far side of what had once been an open fireplace.

'Not exactly the lap of luxury you might have anticipated for your wedding night,' Liam observed, 'but adequate to *our* needs. Do you want to change before dinner?'

'Do I do it in front of you?' she asked.

His shrug held amusement. 'I already have plenty of cigarettes.'

'Then I'll stay as I am.' She was being ridiculous, and she knew it, yet it didn't seem to make any difference. Inevitably the moment would come when she could no longer keep him at arm's length, only until that moment came she refused to give up what little independence she still retained.

The dining room was already quite full for a mid-week evening. They studied the menu in the residents' bar over drinks, had their order taken and were told they would be called when it was prepared.

Jaime wondered what would happen if Tris and Susan took it into their heads to come out here for dinner tonight of all nights. There was no reason why they should choose this one place out of all the others available, of course, but no reason why they shouldn't either. The way fate had been treating her these last few weeks anything could happen. They could hold a party, she thought a little wildly, and wanted suddenly to laugh.

Liam was watching her face, glass in hand. 'That's the first time you've smiled all day,' he remarked. 'Want to share the joke?'

'It wasn't a joke.' She met his gaze and felt her heart turn over in recollection of what they were. Husband and wife. It still didn't seem real. She said, 'I was just thinking how awkward it would be if Tris and Susan turned up here tonight.'

His lips twitched in response. 'Very. I don't think it's one of their usual haunts.'

'They've hardly had time to form any since Susan came back.'

'Well,' he said, 'we'll cross that bridge if we come to it. Would you like a cigarette?'

She started to shake her head, then changed her mind. Smoking might he bad for the health, but it was good for the nerves. 'I might get myself a holder,' she remarked lightly, putting the slim white tube between her lips. 'They're far more elegant.'

'Not your style,' said Liam, and she glanced at him.

'What, elegance?'

This time his smile was genuine. 'I meant too pretentious.'

It was out before she thought about it. 'Isn't that what I'm supposed to be?'

'Different definition.' His eyes had hardened again. 'I'm not going to spend tonight arguing that point over.'

'No,' she said, 'I don't suppose you are.' There was a definite quiver in the hand she used to hold the cigarette steady to his proffered light. She sat back with averted eyes, aware of his mockery and hating him for it. Taking a woman to bed was no novelty to him; why should a wife merit a more tender approach?

She dragged the meal out deliberately, picking at her food with as much appetite as a sparrow. Liam made no attempt to hurry her up, nor to stop her from drinking too much of the excellent wine. It was her own common sense which told her she wasn't going to drink herself into anything but a bad head—or worse. Any alternative had to be better than throwing up on one's wedding night.

Left to keep any conversation going, Liam made a very fair job. He talked about Oakleigh, about when he and Tris were boys; about the travelling he had done as a younger man. The only thing he did not discuss was their future together after this night. That was in the lap of the gods.

By ten-thirty Jaime could procrastinate no longer. In the end it was she herself who suggested they should call it a day, steeling her mind against the growing need in her to try once more to convince him that she was not what he believed. What was the use? He either found proof or he didn't. That was with the gods too.

The bedroom was warm. She went across and opened a window, standing there for a moment or two drawing in breaths of sweet-scented air. When she did turn back, Liam had taken off jacket and tie and was unbuttoning his shirt, the sleeves already free of the gold links.

'I'm neither turning away nor putting the light out,' he stated flatly when she continued to stand without moving at the window. 'Would you rather *I* undressed you?'

Jaime swallowed, her heartbeats like thunder in her ears. 'Yes,' she whispered.

His hands stopped moving, leaving the silk shirt pulled open to the waist and halfway back over his shoulders. Something was altering in his eyes, the hardness melting into a sudden flaring warmth, the lines of his face taking on subtly softer angles. He came to her swiftly, lifting her up and into his arms, finding her mouth in a kiss which brought her every sense springing to life. She clung to him, not caring about anything beyond these moments.

'I love you,' she said with pleading when he let her draw breath for a moment. 'Liam ...'

'It doesn't matter.' His voice was low and rough. 'Not any more. I don't care what happened in the past, Jaime. It's what happens now to both of us that counts. I want you, darling, more than I ever wanted any woman in my life. If I've been brutal with you it's because I couldn't help myself. Jealousy is a soul-destroying thing!'

'I know. I felt that way about Lillian too until I realised you didn't care for her any more.' Her own voice was muffled against his chest. 'Oh, Liam, I wish ...'

'Don't. We're not going to waste any more time wishing—either of us. We're stuck with this place here tonight, but tomorrow we start again from scratch. We can be at Manchester airport inside a couple of hours, and on a plane to anywhere you want to go. No going home till we've had a chance to get to know one another, Jaime. Not just physically but all the way through. You want that too, don't you?'

'Yes. Oh, yes!' It was no time now to be pressing for the one thing he couldn't yet give her. That would come —sooner or later. She lifted her mouth to his, hands behind the dark head holding him close. 'Take me to bed,' she whispered. 'I want you so!'

His arms were gentle now gathering her up, his mouth passionate on hers as he carried her across the room. Jaime gave herself willingly into his hands—this big, domineering brute of a husband she would love all the days of her life.

Best Seller Romances

Next month's best loved romances

Mills & Boon Best Seller Romances are the love stories that have proved particularly popular with our readers. These are the titles to look out for next month.

MARRIAGE IN MEXICO
Flora Kidd

FACTS OF LOVE
Roberta Leigh

DECEIT OF A PAGAN
Carole Mortimer

Buy them from your usual paperback stockist, or write to: Mills & Boon Reader Service, P.O. Box 236, Thornton Rd, Croydon, Surrey CR9 3RU, England. Readers in South Africa-write to: Mills & Boon Reader Service of Southern Africa, Private Bag X3010, Randburg, 2125.

Mills & Boon
the rose of romance

House of Storms
Violet Winspear

Mills & Boon

New from Violet Winspear, one of Mills and Boon's best-selling authors, a longer romance of mystery, intrigue, suspense and love. Almost twice the length of a standard romance for just £1.95. Published on the 14th of June.

Mills & Boon

The Rose of Romance

The perfect holiday romance

ACT OF BETRAYAL
Sara Craven

MAN HUNT
Charlotte Lamb

YOU OWE ME
Penny Jordan

LOVERS IN THE AFTERNOON
Carole Mortimer

Have a more romantic holiday this summer with the Mills & Boon holiday pack.

Four brand new titles, attractively packaged for only £4.40.

The holiday pack is published on the 14th June. Look out for it where you buy Mills & Boon.

Mills & Boon

The Rose of Romance

Mills & Boon

Accept 4 Best Selling Romances Absolutely FREE

Enjoy the very best of love, romance and intrigue brought to you by Mills & Boon. Every month Mills & Boon very carefully select 3 Romances that have been particularly popular in the past and re-issue them for the benefit of readers who may have missed them first time round. Become a subscriber and you can receive six superb novels every two months, and your personal membership card will entitle you to a whole range of special benefits too: a free newsletter, packed with exclusive book offers, recipes, competitions and your guide to the stars, plus there are other bargain offers and big cash savings.

AND an Introductory FREE GIFT for YOU. Turn over the page for details.

As a special introduction we will send you
FOUR superb and exciting
Best Seller Romances – yours to keep Free
– when you complete and return
this coupon to us.

At the same time we will reserve a subscription to Mills & Boon Bestseller Romances for you. Every two months you will receive the 6 specially selected Bestseller novels delivered direct to your door. Postage and packing is always completely Free. There is no obligation or commitment – you can cancel your subscription at any time.

You have absolutely nothing to lose and a whole world of romance to gain. Simply fill in and post the coupon today to:-
MILLS & BOON READER SERVICE, FREEPOST,
P.O. BOX 236, CROYDON, SURREY CR9 9EL.

Please note:- READERS IN SOUTH AFRICA write to
Mills & Boon Ltd., Postbag X3010,
Randburg 2125, S. Africa.

FREE BOOKS CERTIFICATE

To: Mills & Boon Reader Service, FREEPOST, P.O. Box 236, Croydon, Surrey CR9 9EL.

Please send me, free and without obligation, four Mills & Boon Bestseller Romances, and re serve a Reader Service Subscription for me. If I decide to subscribe I shall receive, following my free parcel of books, six new Bestseller Romances every two months for £6.00*, post and pack ing free. If I decide not to subscribe, I shall write to you within 10 days. The free books are mine to keep in any case. I understand that I may cancel my subscription at any time simply by writing to you. I am over 18 years of age.
Please write in BLOCK CAPITALS.

Name _____

Address _____

_____ Postcode _____

SEND NO MONEY — TAKE NO RISKS.

Remember, postcodes speed delivery. Offer applies in UK only and is not valid to present subscribers. Mills & Boon reserve the right to exercise discretion in granting membership. If price changes are necessary you will be notified. Offer expires 31st December 1985.
4BS
* Subject to possible V.A.T.

EP14